The Mermaid's Song

by
Don Conroy

MENTOR

This Edition first published 1998 by

MENTOR PRESS
43 Furze Road,
Sandyford Industrial Estate,
Dublin 18.

Tel. (01) 295 2112/3   Fax. (01) 295 2114

ISBN: 0-947548-98-X

A catalogue record for this book is available from the British Library

Cover Illustration: Don Conroy
Editing, Design and Layout by Mentor Press

Printed in Ireland by ColourBooks Ltd.

1 3 5 7 9 10 8 6 4 2

The most beautiful thing
we can experience is the mysterious

Albert Einstein

The Author

Don Conroy is one of Ireland's most popular writers. He has written many books for children and young adults.

Well-known as an artist, wildlife expert and television personality, Don is actively involved in conservation and environmental work.

Dedicated

to

Avril Duffy

Contents

Chapter	Page
1	11
2	15
3	22
4	30
5	35
6	46
7	52
8	65
9	72
10	77
11	81
12	89
13	98
14	117
15	122
16	137
17	148

Chapter 1

'I heard the voice of the sea; the sound touched my whole being. It was the oldest of voices and the saddest.' Tears welled up inside her eyes and spilled down her face. 'I heard a long melancholy wail . . .' she continued, but the others could see how painful it was for her.

'This was followed by a heavy sobbing. Then a voice sounded in my head. Whispers at first, then I heard it say: "From my womb did I give them life. They take all the treasures my seas yield up, but give back nothing in return." '

The mermaids listened intently. They were startled and confused by the words from the one they called Grandmother Nature.

Emerald gently moved over to the old mermaid and wiped her eyes with her hair. 'Don't be sad,' she whispered tenderly and hugged her.

'It was only a bad dream,' said Azure.

'Come and bathe in the healing waters,' said Jade.

Her three granddaughters helped Grandmother Nature into the rainbow pool.

'Thank you, my children,' said the old mermaid as she eased herself into the pool. 'Ah, that feels so good.' She gave a sigh of relief as she stretched herself out in the enchanting waters.

Emerald removed the mother-of-pearl clip from her grandmother's hair, letting it fall free. Her hair spread out on the surface of the water like grey seaweed. Emerald began to brush it gently.

'That feels so good, my child.'

Jade began to work on her grandmother's hands, gently

massaging them, while Azure cleaned her scaly tail, removing bits of crustaceans and seaweed that had become entangled in her lower body and tail.

The young mermaids could feel the tension wash out of their grandmother's tired body as they continued to massage and groom the old woman. After a time they carried her back to her favourite seat in the cavern. Together they ate a dish of young seaweed shoots.

Then Grandmother Nature spoke again to her grandchildren: 'We must bring the message to the land people, the nusham.'

'But is it not forbidden by mermaid law to have contact with the land people?' said Azure.

'We are living in dangerous times, dear Azure. We need to go beyond the ancient laws in order to save the spirit of the sea. It is the nusham who are out of harmony with the natural law. We must bring this message to them, this warning! That if they do not learn a reverence and respect for the sea, sky, land and all its many inhabitants no matter how big or small, then they are on the road to extinction.'

'What does it matter,' said Jade, 'if they destroy themselves? They act like they are aliens, separate from all wild folk.'

'My dear child, if we lose anything from the sea, sky or land we become the poorer for it. The nusham have developed the deadly powers; if they are not used properly not only will they destroy themselves but all life as we know it as well.'

Emerald gently rubbed the old mermaid's temple.

'My children, time is turning against us. If we fail in this task and our sea world is poisoned then all will perish. I am not really Grandmother Nature,' she smiled, 'I am just an old woman at the close of a rich and wonderful life. I have always

tried to distil and understand the rich wisdom that life offered to me. This strange and beautiful thing we call life, ebbs and flows out of the unfathomable depths – the secret fountain. I do not know how any of us has earned the right of life but since we have it, we must not abuse it. We must make the land people aware that life is sacred.

'How we do this, my children, I do not know. They don't hear the voices of nature pleading with them. They have become deaf to the song of the birds, the call of the whales, the voices on the winds. Their hearts are cold and blocked. How can we unlock their hearts to link them again with wild nature, as their ancient people once did?'

Chapter 2

Emerald woke at dawn. She lay near the surface, listening to the sea washing to the rocky shore. She had slept fitfully. Grandmother Nature's words had spoken in quiet whispers to her all through the night. The words had whipped up her mind to a frenzy, like the way the winter storms whipped up the water. She still had a feeling of dread that followed her from her dreams to her waking state. Her throat seemed to close with fear every time she remembered the words.

Suddenly her friend broke through the surface startling her. The dolphin circled her, then announced his arrival properly with a couple of leaps in the air. He clicked several times and shook his head back and forth, nodding a greeting. She rubbed his pink tongue and his lips. Then, pulling himself into an upright position, he slapped the water with his flippers, made several high pitched sounds, then thrashed the water with his fluke.

Emerald's kind had learned to communicate telepathically with all wild folk. The dolphin was sending sound pictures to her, wanting her to play some aquatic games. She knew, too, that he sensed her mood.

'You want me to play, Dorad?' said Emerald brightly. 'Well, I'm not moving from here until I get my morning kiss.'

The dolphin dipped below the waves, brushing her body with a feather-like touch, then dived deeper. She turned her body to see where he was but he was nowhere to be seen. She twisted and turned, splashing the water with her hands. In an instant the dolphin leaped over her head and crashed down behind her. She turned, only to find Dorad face to face with her. He brushed her cheek with his beak.

Emerald stroked the smooth body of the dolphin. 'That's better,' she said as she pulled him closer to kiss his beak. Then gesturing to him, Dorad began to twirl his body, rotating it several times, then plopped back into the water. The young mermaid climbed onto his back and with her two hands gripped his dorsal fin.

'All aboard,' she shouted.

They sat for a few minutes in the gently heaving swell. Emerald's spirit had soon brightened with the arrival of the dolphin. She watched the golden flow of light tinting the water as it reached out like arms towards them. They communicated in silent reverence with the awakening day for several minutes. The sun now gilded their bodies. The dolphin could feel her soft hands caressing his dorsal fin. He twisted his head from side to side to detect any noise or movement that could spell danger. All was well.

'LOOK!' Emerald called excitedly as she pointed to the sky. They watched a falcon harness the energy of the wind and soar

higher and higher until it was out of view. The dolphin and the mermaid frolicked about for a time, splashing each other. Then they were away, streaking through the water, swimming at full speed, the dolphin effortlessly weaving a zigzag pattern through the sparkling sea.

Emerald gazed down at the speeding form beneath her as he knifed through the water. She remembered, how when she was only a small child, Dorad had sought out her company from all the other mermaids. From then on, a special bond had been forged between them, stronger even than family. He had taught her many things, including how to assimilate knowledge about the wind, the waves and the tides. She reached over and hugged him dearly, running her arms over his body. The dolphin slowed his pace to a gentle porpoising movement.

Breaking the surface of the water Emerald stretched her arms skywards and exclaimed loudly: 'What more could anyone desire but the freedom and beauty of life!'

The dolphin swivelled his head and suddenly dived below the waves.

'What's the matter?' Emerald wondered as she followed him. She stroked his side, sensing his tension.

'A nusham! Walking the beach,' the dolphin communicated.

They both peered above the waves and looked at the lone figure walking along the sandy beach.

'It's the lighthouse keeper,' said Emerald. 'I have seen him many times before. Nothing to fear,' she said brightly. 'I have gone very close to the cove on bright moonlit nights and he has been out sitting on a rock or collecting driftwood. He has never seen me, or if he has, he has taken no notice of me.'

The dolphin made several clicking noises.

'Oh, you're right,' said Emerald. 'We must always be cautious when the nusham are about. But he seems kind enough. In fact I have seen him rescue a cormorant that had been entangled by discarded netting other nusham use for fishing. He released it back to the waters unharmed.'

The dolphin began to circle her. Emerald grabbed onto the dorsal fin and pulled herself up on his back and they were away, leaping over the waves again. Emerald shrieked with delight. The dolphin suddenly came to a halt, nearly sending her flying over his head. She barely managed to hold on.

'That was sneaky,' she scolded as they sat motionless far out to sea. The dolphin shook his head. Emerald became aware of a sounding horn that wailed several times. It was a call she must answer. For it was an urgent message to all mermaids to get to the dome cave immediately.

'We must hurry, something very important is up. That's a distress call!'

The dolphin sped in the direction of the sound, traversing the dazzling light on the sea. They suddenly came upon Jade and Azure who were also playing about with a pod of dolphins.

'I hope everything is all right,' said Jade to Emerald as she arrived alongside them.

'We'll soon find out,' answered Emerald.

Without a moment's delay they hurried to the great cavern. They moved down into dark waters until the dome-shaped caverns loomed up ahead. In single file they moved into the interior channels, past a shipwreck that was now home to the conger eels that peered suspiciously at the mermaids and dolphins as they filed by. Then descending deeper into the hollow chambers and the deep vaulted caverns, they finally reached the inner temple with its massive dome-shaped roof. The basin of the sea.

Emerald looked at all the other mermaids who sat around like statues, watching, waiting. Grandmother Nature lay very still on a bed of seaweed. Emerald's mother and father sat alongside her with the rest of the elders. Emerald climbed from the dolphin and with Jade and Azure they hurried to be alongside their grandmother. They kissed her tenderly. Her eyes remained closed. Her breathing was slow but audible. All around her Emerald could hear a babble of voices, and murmurs of the sea as it gently flowed in and out of the deep crevices.

Suddenly Grandmother Nature opened her eyes. She stared around at the faces, then as if her eyes had come into focus, she reached up her frail arm, hand limply extended, and mustering all her strength she pointed a finger at Emerald.

'My child . . .' Her voice was weak as she repeated the words. 'My child, it is you who must make the journey to the land people, convince them that they are on the road to destruction.' She gasped. There was a rattle in her throat. 'You must warn them that they are dragging all of nature with them down into the abyss.' She gripped Emerald's hand tightly. Emerald trembled uncontrollably.

The old mermaid's grip loosened as she rested back on the soft bed of channel wrack. Her eyelids slowly closed as her life ebbed away. A slow sad sobbing began as the mermaids lamented the passing of their dear Grandmother Nature. Tears flowed freely as bodies rocked to and fro. A chorus of beautiful voices echoed around the large dome and into the deep caves and crevices. Then from one cavern the water bubbled out, creating what appeared as whorls of phosphorescent light that soon grew into waves of pure dazzling light, spilling out and making the mermaids shield their eyes. A light form in the shape of the old mermaid's body rose from her remains and floated into the wave of dazzling light.

'Her soul is now cut adrift from her body,' said Tarmon, as he pointed to the moving shape.

Then the wave of light swept across the dead body, engulfing, then transforming it. The mermaids watched and marvelled at the spectacle which none of the younger members had ever seen before. In front of their very eyes the old mermaid's body changed into pale blue water, which rose up like a pillar, then poured itself into a golden urn which was held by one of the elders. The whorl of dazzling light then suddenly shot out of the cavern like a laser beam.

Emerald and the others looked at each other in utter amazement, finding it very difficult to comprehend what they had just witnessed.

The elder who held the golden urn containing the blue water raised it aloft, bowed her head in silent prayer and said a few prayers, then drank from the urn. When she had done this, she passed it around so everyone might drink from it. When it was finally passed to Emerald she held it anxiously and looked at her parents.

'Drink my child,' said Pearl, her mother. 'In this way your grandmother will always live on within all of us.'

Emerald slowly held the golden urn to her mouth and drank deeply from it. Thoughts of her grandmother floated in her mind — the way she had chosen her as the 'one'. Surely she didn't mean for Emerald to go the nusham and try to persuade them not to destroy the planet? Emerald was not qualified for such a task and were she to do it, it would mean she must forfeit her mermaid form and have a body like the land people.

She caught sight of her mother staring hard at her but said nothing. Then the choir of mermaids began to sing again, filling the air with their beautiful sad songs. Grief welled up inside Emerald and she sobbed uncontrollably.

Chapter 3

Weeks passed.

Emerald sat on a rock looking out to sea, safe in the knowledge that very few nusham vessels visited this tiny island. Cormorants and kittiwakes were her only company. The sun hung low in the sky. All was silent, except for the gentle slapping of the water against the rock, and the bubbling sounds of the seaweed bed. She sorely missed her grandmother. She had been able to talk to her about so many things that she found difficult to discuss with her mother. She loved Pearl dearly but she always seemed so busy and unwilling to engage in long conversations with Emerald.

Pearl was beautiful; her very beauty entranced everyone who came in contact with her. She was once crowned Queen of the Seven Seas. Sometimes Emerald's parents would be away for long periods – there was always a conference, a party, a celebration or a crisis that they would be invited to attend. Emerald didn't envy her mother's popularity or her travels, but she wished she could have the same kind of relationship with her mother that she had with her grandmother.

Jade and Azure seemed to have a better relationship or understanding with her mother than Emerald had. How she longed to be held by her mother and have her whisper: 'It's all right my child, there is nothing to be fearful about. We love you dearly.'

Emerald had expressed her love to her mother in so many ways, but the feeling never seemed to be reciprocated. Once she said to her mother: 'I love you with all my being.'

'I know you do, Emerald,' her mother responded, then asked for her hairbrush to be handed to her.

Do emotions and feelings grow like one's body until they get to be a certain size, then begin to shrink again as one becomes an adult? Emerald wondered.

Tarmon, her father was a kind man but he too seemed unable to show affection. Maybe the price of growing up was that people became less open with their emotions. In that case, Emerald thought, she never wanted to be an adult, if that's the price she had to pay.

Yet she was reminded again of Grandmother Nature who seemed to grow more caring and loving the older she got. Now she was gone and only her seaweed words were left for Emerald to listen to. She began to think of the idea of living with the land people. What a terrible prospect, she thought. Moving away from everything familiar and important to her, to live in an alien world. She began shivering on the rock at the very thought of it.

As she sat shivering Emerald spotted the familiar triangular fin moving through the water, then disappearing. She scanned the water to see where Dorad would appear next. Suddenly he reared overhead making a loud splash as he hit the water. The dozing cormorants nearby quickly took flight, expressing their annoyance at being disturbed.

The dolphin circled, then rising out of the waves vertically he nodded and clicked. Emerald smiled and slipped into the dark waters. With powerful strokes she moved towards Dorad. She rubbed his beak, then his head and felt his blowhole. A jet of water shot from it.

She hugged him tenderly, then stroked his body.

'Dear Dorad, I think you are the only one in the entire world who understands me.'

He thrashed the water with his tail. Suddenly, an idea began to form in Emerald's mind.

'Dorad?' she said in tender tones, 'I want you to accompany me.' The dolphin nodded and clicked. 'To the big island where the nusham live.' The dolphin seemed anxious. 'You're not afraid, Dorad?' The dolphin clicked several times. 'You're afraid for me, but there is no need to be,' Emerald reassured him. 'We will have the cloak of night to conceal us.' Dorad clicked again. 'That's very sweet of you, dear Dorad. I know you would do anything for me.'

Emerald and Dorad slowly swam towards the island. The light from the lighthouse was shining out to sea like a welcoming beacon. As they got closer to shore Emerald could feel her heart pounding. Yet all was clear. There was no one on the beach or along the cliffs. The warm light was coming from the lighthouse keeper's house. After they had circled the water beneath the cliffs and rested for a time on the rocks, the dolphin signalled to leave.

'But, Dorad, I've come this close many times before. I want to make the journey up the river to see the interior,' pleaded Emerald.

The dolphin shook his head furiously.

The young mermaid held Dorad's large head in her hands. 'I won't go far, just up a little way. Do you want to stay here and catch your supper? I promise to return before the stars are extinguished from the sky.'

The dolphin exhaled loudly.

'I know you think I'm foolish, but sometimes I get this great desire to explore life. If I could I would swim to the moon just to view our world from there. Have you never wondered about the land people?'

The dolphin made several clicking noises.

'There you are,' said Emerald. 'I know some of your kind have gone out to seek contact with the nusham. Well that's what I want to do. I've decided I want to cross the threshold and encounter these strange beings. It's what my grandmother desired from me. You saw her, on her deathbed pointing to me. No, Dorad, I'm not going to live with them tonight. Something like that takes lots of planning. I don't know how I could move comfortably around on land with this tail of mine. That's why I need to explore what it is like to move up a river like the salmon.'

The dolphin clicked and nudged her.

'I know I'm not a salmon, cheeky!' She gripped his beak tightly. 'Are you coming or not?'

The dolphin agreed to travel up the river with his companion.

Emerald finned a short way up the coast to where the river meets the sea. The dolphin went behind her and began to propel her through the water faster and faster. Emerald shrieked with laughter as she was pushed through the water. When they reached the mouth of the river, Emerald began to make her way slowly inland. The air was soft and warm. The brackish water seemed thinner and easier to move through. There was no great depth to the river although it was quite wide. The water was only about waist high when Emerald pulled herself into an upright position.

A beautiful image passed them by on the far side of the river. The mute swan had spied the two creatures earlier and came to investigate them at a safe distance. She hissed when she saw the dolphin and quickly made a return and hurried back up river. They watched the ghostly form make her way to the safety of a distant reed bed. In the distance there was the sound of hooves as several horses raced and played in the quiet fields.

'Isn't this very exciting?' said Emerald as she put her arm around Dorad.

The dolphin clicked his disapproval and suggested they return before any nusham would see them.

Lights pierced the darkness and the sound of a car startled Emerald. It came to a halt near a stone bridge. A window in the car was rolled down and Emerald could see two figures. They were the nusham. A female voice could be heard as her laughter broke the silence. Music came from the car. Then one of the nusham got out of the car and walked over to the river. Emerald and Dorad quickly ducked down below the surface. They were both unaware how shallow the water had become.

The man looked down into the river and when he saw the dorsal fin he yelled loudly: 'Jill, come here quickly. Jill,' he yelled even more loudly.

The girl got out of the car and shouted back. 'What is it?'

'I think there's a shark in the water,' he said nervously.

'Don't be cracked in the head,' she said laughing loudly. 'Fancy a shark in a river.' She adjusted the back strap on her shoe as she moved closer.

'Well, come and see for yourself. Wait a minute, get my camera. It's in the glove compartment.' The girl turned back to get the camera. Emerald's heart was pounding as she tried to flatten out her slender body on the riverbed. The dolphin raised his head and could see a shadowy image of another nusham on the other side of the riverbank. But the angler didn't see anything and moved downriver to find a better spot.

'Quick,' yelled the young man to his girlfriend.

'I'm hurrying,' she complained as the audio tapes fell from the glove compartment while she searched for the camera.

Emerald got a terrific urge to sneeze but tried to stifle it. The dolphin clicked a warning call. Emerald sneezed loudly and raised her head out of the water. The young man got such a shock when he saw the beautiful form of the mermaid rise out of the shallow water, followed by the dolphin raising his head, that he slipped on the dewy grass. Losing his footing he fell down the bank into the water.

Emerald and Dorad quickly turned and torpedoed down the river back to the safety of the sea.

'Smile,' said the girl, as she clicked the camera button and laughed uncontrollably. The young man sat in the water completely soaked while the angler on the opposite bank hurried across the water to pull him out.

'Did you see?' the young man stammered.

'What?' asked the angler trying to support him.

'A dolphin and a mermaid right here swimming in the river.'

The angler laughed. 'I've been on the river these past two hours and I haven't seen a fish, let alone a dolphin! I wouldn't mind seeing a mermaid though.'

'Come on, Eddie. We'll get you home,' smiled Jill as she linked her arm in his and walked him back to the car.

'But it's true . . . I'm telling you . . . every word . . .'

'Thanks for your help,' Jill called to the angler. 'Just as well it wasn't any deeper. Eddie can't swim,' she laughed again.

The angler raised his hat. 'It was my pleasure. Safe home,' he added.

'I hope you catch a big one,' she shouted after him as she helped Eddie into the car. 'I'll drive,' she said cheerfully.

'It's true!' Eddie insisted. 'I'm telling you, I saw what I saw.'

Jill handed him a tissue to wipe the water from his face. She laughed loudly as she started up the engine. Soon they were away down the country road.

Emerald chuckled broadly: 'Dear Dorad, let's head home. I think we've had enough excitement for one evening.' She climbed onto his back and they raced away over the waves.

Chapter 4

They swam all night in the starry darkness and by early dawn they were nearing home. Emerald spied something bobbing up ahead. As they moved closer, a head raised from the water.

'Lutra!' Emerald exclaimed, as the leathery turtle surfaced briefly.

A long rope trailed from the turtle's right front flipper. The dolphin moved swiftly alongside the turtle. Emerald leaped from the dolphin into the water.

'Dear Lutra, how are you?'

The turtle seemed a little startled, then recognised his dear friends. Emerald closed her eyes and turned to the turtle. Soon they were communicating in a telepathic way.

'Of course I'll remove this rope.' She answered Lutra's request and unwound the rope that had been wrapped around the flipper several times. The rope had bitten deeply into the skin.

'I'm becoming careless in my old age,' the turtle declared when he was at last free from the lobsterpot rope. It's happened to me before, you know.'

Emerald asked how he was, as she had not seen him for over two years.

'Well as could be expected at my age,' he grinned. 'You run the gauntlet when you are a seafarer like me. It's getting more dangerous each season.' He gave a deep sigh. 'I've seen wild folk mangled by propellers and strangled by discarded fishing nets. I've seen trawling nets drown thousands of creatures, whales, dolphins, sharks, turtles, seals, fish . . . quite shocking really. Then those dredgers that crush everything in sight, a lot of senseless death,' he sighed. 'Ah but listen to me, I've only met you a moment and I'm complaining.'

Emerald smiled and kissed him on the top of the head and rubbed his carapace, which was soft to the touch apart from the long ridges that ran from the shoulders to the tail.

The sea mirrored the dawn as it caught the sun's first light, turning the water to a rose colour. The group of three moved slowly and gracefully through the water. Emerald was greatly pleased to have the company of the old turtle again. Lutra was always full of wonderful stories about the far off oceans. Once he had even brought her a necklace which he had found in a wreck. It was studded with rubies and diamonds. He said it must have belonged to a beautiful princess from the ancient world; now he was giving it to the princess of the sea.

Emerald had been so happy to receive the necklace. She remembered her sisters being a little jealous at the time. But the turtle had brought them gifts of bracelets and rings on previous occasions. Emerald offered the necklace to her mother but she declined it, saying she had trunks full of jewellery that had been given to her by various mermen, mermaids and sea creatures, including Lutra. Emerald only wore the necklace on special occasions.

Dorad had given her many gifts too; one was a pearl necklace that she wore across her forehead most days. The dolphin suggested they should visit Grypus, the old seal, since they were near his island. In the distance it loomed ahead out of the sea, its rocks rising in jagged splendour.

'You've read my mind,' said Lutra.

Emerald was always willing to meet new acquaintances, although she had heard so much about the old seal, Grypus, from her mother and grandmother that she felt she knew him already. Her mother told her that he had been one of the distinguished guests at her first birthday celebrations.

They moved in the calm waters in unison. They could see the old seal holding himself in an upright position near the tide line. He barked a loud greeting as they approached the shore. 'What a wonderful surprise to see you all.' Grypus moved into the water, making a loud splash as he hastened to meet them.

'Greetings, old friend,' said Lutra. 'You know Emerald?'

'Indeed I do,' snorted Grypus. 'Give these old bones a hug.' Emerald threw her arms around the heavy bulk. 'The last time I saw you, my child, you were a beautiful baby. Now you're a beautiful young lady.'

The dolphin nudged the old seal. Old Grypus turned around. 'Ah my dear Dorad.'

'It's been a long time, too long,' said Dorad as they splashed each other in a friendly fashion.

The four of them spent the morning regaling each other with stories of the past. Emerald felt good in their company. By mid-morning Dorad suggested a visit to a kelp forest he knew to be nearby. They dropped below the surface and followed Dorad to the hidden grove. Lutra and Grypus admitted they never had been there before. As the group moved with the greatest of ease through the swirls of kelp, Emerald pulled herself from stalk to stalk pausing to look around.

'The kelp provides sustenance and shelter for so many forms of life,' said Lutra. 'The giant kelp can grow two feet a day. Many grow up to a hundred feet or more,' he added.

Emerald marvelled as she roamed excitedly about. Dorad seemed to be in ecstasy as he brushed his body along the stalks and the long leathery fronds.

'Try it,' he suggested to the others. They too experienced the healing powers of the kelp forest.

Not to be outdone by Dorad, Grypus requested that they visit a special place of his that few knew about.

'Oh I love discovering new places like this one,' said Emerald, stroking the dolphin along his side.

Leaving the towering grove of kelp, old Grypus stopped. 'First things first,' he said. They returned to the surface to breathe. 'Aah, that's better,' said the old seal, as he took in gulps of fresh moist air. He blinked his big eyes and twitched his long whiskers. They all felt better after replenishing their air. 'Now that we are all feeling invigorated, let's go to see my special place.'

Lutra chuckled to himself as he had been to Grypus' secret place several times, but Grypus probably didn't remember showing it to him. Emerald picked up on this and winked at the old turtle.

They slipped just beneath the surface and moved through the pristine water, their bodies lapped by the glimmering waves as they stroked for the old seal's secret place. Silvery shoals passed below them and shearwaters were weaving in and out of the waves up ahead of them. Swooping gulls could be seen in the distance following a fishing trawler. Visibility was perfect. Below on the sea floor meadows of underwater vegetation moved to the gentle ebb and flow of the currents. The water was teeming with life.

Chapter 5

From the sunlit surface water Emerald gazed at the vegetation below, remembering that Grandmother Nature had told her how plants use the sunlight to make their food in a process called photosynthesis. She then spied a lesser-spotted dogfish moving around the seabed searching for shellfish and crustaceans. It was a male; perhaps his mate had gone to the shallow waters to lay her eggs individually among the swaying seaweed. How many times Emerals had collected these rectangular capsules with their four corners when she was a child. Her grandmother called these egg cases 'mermaid purses'. Emerald remembered finding her first one and how she hurried back to her clan asking if any of the mermaids or mermen had lost their purse. She recalled her father and the elders laughing loudly when she produced the case. She was very indignant with them at the time. Now it made her smile broadly at the idea. Of course it was a story that was always dredged up on special occasions, when her father or her sisters would recount the incident.

'Nearly there,' said Grypus as they dived below a sea shelf. He porpoised ahead of the others. 'Well, what do you think?' He circled about feeling very pleased with himself. Ahead lay a sunken vessel, an old liner.

'It's probably as old as me,' said Lutra, moving gracefully closer to the hull of the ship. Emerald sensed an eerie atmosphere about the place, but the others didn't seem to be too perturbed. They swam about, venturing in and out of the old ship's gaping holes. The vessel had become an artificial reef with algae encrusted on its steel frame and coral and sponges ornamenting the hull. In turn these creatures would provide food for other marine life forms.

Emerald had seen shipwrecks before but never anything as large as this. It was extraordinary how the sea could transform the nusham's discarded ship, make it look like a reef, and have it teeming with life. She looked at Lutra who spied a jellyfish pulsating to the surface. The old turtle chased after it and chomped on it with his powerful jaws.

'You're making me hungry,' said Grypus to Lutra, watching him polish off the moonjelly. 'Not that I could eat that,' he shuddered at the thought of it. A large shoal of sand eels whizzed by. 'Dorad and I are going for a spot of late breakfast,' said Grypus. 'Will you be all right?' he asked Emerald.

'Go,' said Emerald. 'I'll be fine.'

The old seal knew that, with such a large shoal of sand eels around, shoals of mackerel would soon arrive on the scene. He wasn't interested in the smaller fish, but he wouldn't mind a few mackerel. Usually the mackerel preyed on the sand eel, which they caught late at night when the sand eel were feeding on the plankton. The sand eel would run the gauntlet, from common sandwich terns, guillemots, and puffins that had hungry young to feed. Even the dainty paddling kittiwake would take their share.

Within minutes the mackerel had appeared. Dorad and Grypus chased after them in the hope of securing breakfast. Emerald was amused when she thought how Grypus couldn't wait to show her his hidden place but as soon as he saw the shoals of mackerel he couldn't resist chasing after them in the hopes of catching a few.

Lutra stayed with Emerald and they explored the sunken liner. With Lutra ahead, Emerald could admire what a powerful swimmer the turtle really was, his long broad flippers propelling him at great speed through the water. Emerald caught up and swam alongside him.

They came to a tear in the side of the ship. Emerald decided to enter. Moving inside, she gave out a loud shriek. A luminescent shape appeared out of the darkness and a lion's mane jellyfish pulsated past her. She swerved to avoid the stinging tentacles. Lutra saw what happened and homed in on the jellyfish as it made its way to the surface. The turtle grabbed the jellyfish in his jaws. Emerald watched as the tentacles brushed Lutra's body. He was obviously immune to their poisonous sting. Within minutes he had made a meal of the jellyfish.

'Are you all right?' he asked, returning to Emerald's side.

'Oh, fine. It just gave me a shock. I wasn't expecting it. You really enjoy eating jellyfish?' Emerald asked aghast.

'Oh yes,' said the turtle. 'I follow them as they are carried along by the Gulf Stream to these waters.'

'Where did you come from, Lutra?' Emerald asked. 'If it's not too personal a question,' she added.

'Indeed not,' said Lutra. 'I was born in a place called French Guiana, along the South American coast. I've been a regular visitor to these waters over the years along with my other cousins: the loggerhead, the hawkesbill, the kemp's ridley and the green. They make the journey following the warm waters of the Gulf Stream. I suppose the loggerhead would be the most frequent visitor to these waters.'

'I've seen them,' said Emerald proudly. 'On rare occasions, I may add. But you look a bit different from them.'

'Well of course I do,' said Lutra. 'For a start I'm bigger, and I don't have the bony shell with those fancy plates on the carapace like the others. I get my name from the leathery skin on my carapace.'

'Have you a family of your own?' Emerald probed.

'Well, I did have the most beautiful mate you are ever likely to see in the Atlantic. But . . .' he sighed, 'that was a long time ago.'

'Where is she now?' wondered Emerald

'Sadly she was killed by one of those things that help move small boats through the water. A propeller, that's the thing.'

'I'm sorry,' said Emerald.

'Thank you,' said Lutra. 'That was a long time ago, probably before you were born. But I still miss her. She was a wonderful mother and there are a number of our offspring somewhere out there in the azure blue waters.'

Emerald threw her arms around his neck then gently rubbed the reptile along his underside.

'I remember what a graceful swimmer she was. She could go to the great depths of the ocean floor and it didn't bother her. While I was dozing in some cave she would always be off exploring our watery world, travelling to depths of 1200 metres with temperatures almost freezing. That was Leala for you.'

'That was her name, Leala?'

'Yes,' said Lutra. There was a mixture of joy and sadness in his voice. 'I remember one evening . . . it's as if it was only yesterday,' he sighed. 'We'd just had our fill of the jellyfish that swarmed nearby and we were frolicking about. The sun had slipped behind distant hills. The water was burnished in a pale blue light. It wasn't long before the stars appeared. She told me it was her time, that she would swim to the quiet beach and there lay her eggs. I wanted to join her. She was so young, so beautiful. But that was not the turtle way, she reminded me. She told me to go and she would search me out on some warm night like this one, under the stars. Her nickname for me,' he chuckled, 'was Nomad. Which was very apt, I suppose, since I'm always wandering.'

'What happened then?' asked Emerald.

'We said our farewells and I watched as she headed for the lonely shore. You see, we reptiles cannot lay our eggs in the water. The embryo inside each egg would only perish. Of course she would not be the only one making the journey. Other females full with eggs would be on the same quest to bury their eggs in the warm dry sand. I remember watching her at a distance, as she pulled her heavy frame out onto the land. In the water we turtles can move about with no difficulty, but when we are on land it's another story, we are so awkward. The beach she chose was, of course, a favourite place for female turtles to bury their eggs. It's called a rookery.'

'Just like the seals,' added Emerald.

'That's right,' said Lutra.

'Please continue,' said Emerald. 'It's fascinating.'

'Well, after she had dug a deep hole in the sand, she deposited her eggs and covered them with sand. Then she returned to the water exhausted. I wanted to join her but I knew the other females wouldn't approve of a male near them at this time.'

'Do the eggs not need looking after?' asked Emerald.

'No, nature does the rest. The eggs get heat and air through the sand. Soon they all hatch and the hatchlings head in their hundreds for the sea. Many don't make it, of course, with birds, nusham, and even sharks ready to pick them off. But that's the way of nature, sometimes it appears hard, other times

gentle, but there is a great divine plan behind it all, I'm sure of that,' said Lutra.

'You really think so?' Emerald asked, remembering her grandmother's recent death.

'We have our land cousins,' Lutra said brightly. 'They are called tortoises. They live in warmer climates than here. It is said our ancestors are descended from them. Some tortoises took to the sea millions of years ago and became turtles like me. Of course I cannot remember that far back. I'm old,' he added, 'but not that old.' He chuckled. 'It's time to go exploring again before Grypus returns and thinks we're not interested in his secret place.'

Emerald agreed and began to investigate the sunken rusting hulk, passing over a profusion of marine algae and colourful anemones. A conger eel lurking in a dark section peered out, its mouth gaping, then returned to its hiding spot. Emerald went back into the gutted section and swam down the dark recesses of the great structure, weaving in and out of the vast steel caverns, passing by portholes then moving along narrow passages.

She looked at the crumbling wooden structures. A piano that was once used to entertain and bring merriment stood silent, rusting and slowly disintegrating. On entering another area she saw something underneath several rotting doors that had fallen from their frames. It was an old chest wedged tightly under a metal bed frame. Emerald decided to investigate. She pulled at the rusting metal frames until they fell away. A cloud of dust and sand from the debris bubbled up. Emerald brushed at the muddy water with her hands and then proceeded to pull the heavy chest out into a clearing. Small fish swam by; a baby octopus that was hiding nearby crawled to a different position and then went into a corner.

There was movement behind her. Emerald quickly turned around, and there was Lutra heading up the darkened passageway to join her. Emerald indicated to Lutra what she had discovered. She bent down and pulled at the lock that came away in her hand. Gently she lifted the lid of the chest. Inside several objects were visible. Emerald rummaged through the contents of the chest. Papers and letters floated up and moved away in the gentle currents. Emerald caught hold of a postcard.

'They're the pyramids of ancient Egypt,' said Lutra. She looked at them in amazement. 'The nusham built them thousands of years ago,' he added. Another postcard revealed the Eiffel Tower. Then there were old photographs of a man

41

and a woman. The man was wearing a white suit. His hair was parted in the centre and he wore a thick moustache curled at the sides. The young woman looked very beautiful, Emerald thought. As she fingered the surface of the photograph, it began to come away at her touch.

Another photograph showed the same young woman, only this time instead of a blouse and skirt she was wearing a swimsuit. Then there were pictures of older men and women. Emerald imagined they must be the couple's parents. The final picture revealed a small baby with big eyes staring out from the photograph. Emerald felt sad to think they all may have been drowned with the sinking of the liner.

More searching revealed an ivory figurine of a naked young girl. Emerald fingered the delicate object and admired the fine carving. Holding it to her cheek, she felt the coldness of the ivory. Lutra lay on the floor of the hull, resting and watching Emerald as she looked in such wonder at the different objects.

Then her eye noticed something else. She carefully placed the figurine down on the floor and took out an object that was wrapped in a red velvet purse. Opening the purse she fingered inside and pulled out a brooch. She rubbed it with the velvet, then swirled it in the water with her hand to remove the particles of sand and dust. What she was holding was a beautiful and intricately jewelled brooch of diamonds and sapphires.

Then Lutra spied what looked like a small leg under some rubble. He moved over and nudged it, then with his front flipper he scooped it out from its hidden position. Emerald turned to see and then swam down to the object. She held it in her hands; it was a doll. The head was broken and an arm was missing, but there was a strange feeling from it, as if the doll held a mysterious intimacy. Pictures flashed up in Emerald's mind of the couple in the photograph presenting it to their young child, then the little girl hugging and kissing the doll.

Emerald couldn't explain why or how she got the images. But it had happened before when she touched certain objects. Her grandmother had the same gift of second sight. Emerald remembered the times when she made an unexpected visit to her grandmother and the old mermaid always knew it was her, not Azure or Jade. She would say: 'Welcome Emerald,' before she had even entered the cavern.

It was strange indeed, thought Emerald. Maybe some of my grandmother's gifts are being passed on to me. Of course mermaids and mermen were a bit like other wild folk. They could sense things. They could read the water currents and the clouds for weather changes and they knew when ships were approaching. But it took concentration. If one wasn't concentrating or was too occupied with other things, boats could come too close for comfort.

Emerald had heard that some mermaid clans could turn at will into seals or dolphins if danger was near. While her kind had no such powers, they had the ability to appear almost transparent in the water if there was a threat of danger.

'There you are!' The booming voice of Grypus startled her. 'Having fun?' enquired the old seal. 'Sorry we left like that, instinctive reaction you know.'

'Sometimes the stomach rules the head,' Emerald smiled. 'This place is truly fascinating,' she said. 'Thank you for bringing me here.'

'Well, now I think we should go back to my island,' Grypus suggested. They left the silent ship and headed for the surface, Emerald carrying the brooch and the ivory figurine.

As they reached the surface to gulp the air there was a freshening breeze blowing. In the distance oystercatchers flew low over the sea. A pair of gannets circled and wheeled high in the sky. Dorad moved ahead, cruising in energetic undulations over the wavelets. Grypus' shape seemed to change as he too moved forward trying to catch up with the dolphin. His body appeared more streamlined and there was a wonderful fluidity in his movement, his long dog-like snout knifing through the water.

Lutra spurted ahead, proving how fast a swimmer he could be, trying to outpace Grypus. Emerald brushed her hair back from her eyes, her head bobbed just above the water. In the distance across the sparkling azure blue sea she could see the big island with its lonely lighthouse built out on the cliffs. To one side lay the long stretch of quiet beach, with white sand where the waters lapped gently to the shore. The wind drifted and the sound of nesting seabirds could be heard. The kittiwakes were the most vocal from the cliffs. In the water, huge rafts of birds moved about: puffins, razorbills and guillemots. She watched some puffins flying in tight formation, their beaks full of sand eels for their hungry youngsters.

Looking ahead she could still see Dorad racing across the water followed by the others. Overhead on quivering wings, sandwich terns hovered, before diving into the sea. They too were feeding on the large shoals of sand eels. Emerald slipped below the surface and propelled herself at great speed through the water. Kicking strongly and splashing she was soon gaining on her friends. She, too, wanted to show her prowess underwater as she moved with a smooth determined motion through the water. She surfaced again to check on her friends. The dolphin repeatedly leaped out of the water, slapping the surface as he re-entered. Emerald smiled. She knew they were all showing off to each other. There was certainly a friendly rivalry between them, she thought.

Emerald heard movement behind her as a large volume of water was displaced. She dipped below the surface to encounter huge jaws, gaping wide and heading straight for her. She shrieked loudly, then realised it was only a basking shark. Although it was a formidable-looking creature she knew it was perfectly harmless. It moved slowly just below the surface as it sieved the water for plankton. As it passed, she ran her hand along the five gill slits on the side of its head. The rest of its body felt coarse to the touch. The shark didn't take any notice of the young mermaid, being too occupied with feeding.

Emerald loved to see this gentle giant of the sea. Twelve metres long and weighing four tonnes, the basking shark was becoming a rare sight in the area. Surfacing again she could see only the floppy dorsal fin as it cut along the surface of the water, hiding the massive bulk below.

Then another dorsal fin could be seen cutting through the water at great speed. This one belonged to Dorad who had hurried back when he heard the young mermaid's shriek. Realising it was only a basking shark, he circled Emerald and mocked her by splashing her with water.

'Well, it did give me a start,' she scolded the dolphin, pretending to be annoyed. Dorad beckoned her to climb onto him, which she did, gripping his firm dorsal fin tightly. He moved through the water at lightning speed.

Chapter 6

Soon they were back at Grypus' island. The old seal had
already hauled himself out of the water and was lounging
across some boulders, his hind flippers raised above his body.
Lutra was on the sandy patch near where the water lapped the
shore. Emerald climbed off the dolphin onto a barnacle-
encrusted rock. Dorad stuck part of his body out of the water
and onto a clump of bladder wrack that was growing on some
of the outer rocks.

'You haven't eaten, my child,' said Grypus.

'Oh, I don't feel hungry,' said Emerald, checking her tail for
bits of algae or sand that might have stuck to her. Peering into
the water she watched some barnacles. They were feeding
below the waterline, snatching the plankton with their feathery
arms. Mussels and sea squirts too were sucking in the water and
filtering it for plankton. Sea anemone tentacles gently waved
and groped for their meal of plankton. Emerald marvelled how

the almost invisible organisms could feed the giants of the sea, the whale and the basking shark, and feed these tiny creatures as well. 'Nature's great bounty,' she thought to herself.

'You must keep up your strength,' said the old seal. 'I knew there was no point in us catching you a mackerel or a cod. You don't eat that sort of thing.'

Emerald eased herself over to a rock pool and took some green seaweed from it. A blenny darted for cover. Emerald began to pull the algae apart and eat small mouthfuls.

'Well, tell me,' said Grypus, 'how is dear Murgen?'

Emerald adjusted her position. She crouched, with her tail raised, then she let it hang into the water, gently swaying it below the splashing waves. She was silent as tears welled up inside her. 'I'm afraid Murgen's gone, she passed over,' Emerald said sadly.

Grypus shifted awkwardly. He was surprised he hadn't heard. He prided himself on knowing all the important news around, whether good or bad.

'She'll be sorely missed,' said Lutra.

'Indeed,' said Grypus. 'Well, at least she lived to a ripe old age,' he added.

'That's true,' said Emerald wiping the tears that escaped down her cheeks. 'But Grandmother Nature was sad when she was dying, not because of herself, but because she believed that the seas may be dying too.'

Grypus snorted and twitched his whiskers, not quite sure how to respond.

'We called Murgen Grandmother Nature,' said Emerald. 'It was as if she really was the voice of the sea, full of wisdom.'

'Her sister is like that too,' said Lutra.

Emerald looked surprised. She had heard about her

grandmother having a sister, but she knew she lived far away beyond the ocean. 'Tell me about her, please.'

'Well, she was very like her sister, they could almost be mistaken for twins,' said Lutra.

'A regular visitor to these shores,' said Grypus.

'I've never met her,' said Emerald. The dolphin hadn't either.

'Before your time,' Grypus blurted. Then he added: 'Maybe not that regular.'

'Why did she leave?' Emerald asked.

'Well, her wisdom was needed where the ocean meets the distant lands.'

'It's called America,' Lutra added. 'There she was crowned Empress of the Sea, as your grandmother was crowned the same here many moons ago. Her name is Moruadh,' he added.

Emerald wondered if Moruadh knew of the death of her sister, Murgen, and if so why was she not at her death bed. 'Perhaps she is too old to travel,' Emerald thought.

The young mermaid was amazed she hadn't known more about her grandmother's sister before.

'Well, you do now,' said Dorad.

'If you don't ask, you won't find out,' said Grypus.

Then he remembered some of the words Murgen had spoken to him.

'She said the nusham had upset the balance of nature. If they continued on their course they would empty the seas of all life. That they now held the power and maybe the decisive force for the future as to whether wild folk should live or die.'

Lutra recalled her words too saying:

'The nusham think all their connections with nature are cut. They think their technology has lifted them above nature. But the seas must live. That was her message. How can we awaken the nusham to the great mystery called life. Must the seas be sacrificed on the altar of greed and ignorance.'

'No!' shouted Emerald. 'It cannot happen, it must not happen.' The fires of anger raged inside her.

'Calm yourself, my dear,' said Grypus. 'I know these words are harrowing, but your grandmother could feel things that are beyond most of us. You mustn't concern yourself too much, nature will find a way. We are still lucky in these parts; not too many problems. The sea is still pure and teeming with life.'

Emerald recovered herself and then relaxed in the knowledge that she knew now what she must do, no matter how dangerous or painful. There was a long silence. Then Dorad asked Emerald to sing to them. Grypus pleaded too, saying it would relax his aching muscles.

Emerald broke into a broad smile. Her pearly white teeth flashed brightly. 'Come over here,' she said to the old seal, 'and I'll give you a massage while I sing for you all.' Opening her mouth she sounded a few clear notes. Then she took a deep breath and sang. Her voice was so beautiful it seemed to echo about the waves.

It was an apt song, after hearing the words of her grandmother spoken by her friends. It was called *Do not fill the sea with tears*. Her voice was so pure and clear and the words so melancholy.

As she finished the last line of the song with the words 'Let the sea wash the despair from my heart,' a horn sounded. None of them had heard it, they were too enchanted by Emerald's beautiful voice.

Grypus' eyes moistened. 'That was wonderful my dear Emerald, and my muscles feel renewed from your healing touch.'

The horn sounded again. This time there was no mistaking it. It was the call of the mermaids. It sounded a third time.

'This can only mean something very important,' said Emerald.

'Luckily the sound seems to be beyond the reach of the nusham ears,' said Dorad. 'Otherwise your clan would be discovered.'

The horn wailed once again. Emerald thought it was more ominous this time. It made her shudder.

'Look!' said Grypus.

Shapes could be seen porpoising far out to sea. Again the sounding horn could be heard, the sound shivering in the air.

'I must go,' said Emerald. 'Something is about to happen.'

With that her two sisters surfaced. 'Emerald where have you been? We've been searching everywhere for you. You must come immediately,' chorused Azure and Jade.

Emerald dived from the rock into the water, then turning, she called to her friends: 'Sorry I have to go, but it's obviously very important whatever it is.'

Suddenly there in front of her eyes were her mother and father, sitting on two pilot whales that were coming around the island. 'My child, come with us at once. There is a clan meeting of immense importance.' Then looking at the seal, the turtle and the dolphin, Emerald's mother said warmly: 'Perhaps you would like to come as well; you could add your experience and wisdom to the proceedings.'

'We'll be delighted to,' said Grypus.

Lutra and Dorad nodded their agreement. They watched as mermaids, mermen, Suires and Merrows swam by, and among them orcas, pilot whales, dolphins, porpoises, and several hump-backed whales.

Next came a giant blue whale with a grey-haired old woman sitting on top, dressed in green and gold.

'In all my days I've never seen anything like it,' Grypus exclaimed.

'We'd better follow them,' said Lutra.

They slipped quietly into the water.

Chapter 7

Down into the eerie shipwreck with its wooden carvings they moved, into caverns with their tall twisted columns decorated with fossils and shells. There were stairways against the cliffs, worn shiny by centuries of water flow. Painted mythical figures dressed the walls. They journeyed through steep crevices that split the plateau. A bridge joined two wide caves. Tall granite and limestone rocks stood like sentinels, adorned with strange carvings.

In the royal mermaid palace the wild folk had gathered. There was a sense of expectation, of tension. Yet they had all travelled from near and far for this summit. Some spoke quietly among themselves of alarmist talk and were of the opinion that a lot of the dire plight of the sea was mere scare-mongering.

Others thought it was a conspiracy by the nusham to systematically exploit and destroy all marine life. Some claimed they had heard the nusham words from their ships and boats saying: 'If we don't get our share someone else will.' There were those who had seen terrible things. And others whose relatives had been maimed or even destroyed by the nusham activity.

Emerald, Azure and Jade sat high up on a salt column to get a good view. Grypus, Dorad and Lutra stayed below them. A large male orca moved near to Grypus, who got a terrible start. Surely in the Royal Marine Palace all creatures were on neutral ground and it was forbidden for any creature to attack another. The orca was almost touching the old seal.

Grypus was about to growl at him to keep off when he realised that it was the same orca that had rescued his grandson Saoirse from the dreaded black seals.

'How are you, dear Grypus?'

'Oh, well as can be expected,' said the old seal. 'I'm not getting any younger.'

'It's good to see you,' said the orca.

'Likewise,' said Grypus. 'And I'm glad to say we've had little or no trouble from killer whales in these parts.'

'I gave you my word back then, when I returned your grandson to you, that you would not have any problems from our pod. By the way, how is your grandson?'

'Oh fine,' said Grypus. 'As far as I know. Off travelling the world, a bit of a nomad, like Lutra here,' nodding to the turtle, 'but he'll settle some time. He has a wonderful companion called . . .'

'Seafra,' said the turtle.

'Ah yes,' said Grypus. 'Seafra comes from a good colony.'

'I'm glad,' said the orca.

Their conversation was interrupted by the ceremonial horns being blown by the mermen.

Tarmon and Pearl moved to the throne and invited everyone to sit, or take up suitable resting positions. Emerald stared at her mother who was dressed beautifully for the occasion. Her dark hair coiled down to her left shoulder with pearls. Several bracelets of pearls, sapphires, diamonds and rubies dressed her arms. She looked around and noticed her daughters sitting high up on a white column. She parted her lips wide and smiled at them. Her perfect white teeth gleamed through her ruby lips.

Tarmon stood alongside her. He smiled too but it was more strained. Emerald could always tell when he was tense despite his attempts to conceal it. Her father wore a ceremonial gold scallop-shaped gorge around his neck. In his right hand he held the fork of Neptune, which had been handed down for generations to mermen or mermaids who had served the sea community either by performing some heroic deed or shown great compassion or wisdom in times of trouble.

Pearl, always poised, dignified, regal and remote, addressed the many visitors. Some had journeyed from the polar seas, others from the Tropics. Whether they had come from mighty rivers, lakes or oceans they were all welcome and it was hoped their stay would be an enjoyable one. She promised an evening of music and entertainment for all.

'But first,' she said, 'I must introduce a dear relation and friend to us all, Moruadh. Please give her a welcome fitting for an empress.'

The crowds broke into loud cheering and slapping of tails. Seals, dolphins, octopus, whales, sharks and other creatures of the deep threshed the water with flippers, fins, flukes, tentacles and tails. The mighty blue whale moved slowly through the cavern with the old empress sitting astride its head. On seeing her, the crowds grew louder in their appreciation of this frail old mermaid. She was assisted to the throne. When she raised her right hand feebly, the crowds became silent. Despite her obvious frailty she sat with much composure. On either side of her were Tarmon and Pearl.

A shiver of awe came over Emerald as she gazed up at Moruadh. She looked so like Murgen it was uncanny. Looking around Emerald noted that the corridors of the palace were packed with visitors, all wishing to get a glimpse of the old mermaid and listen to the pearls of wisdom that would issue from her.

Moruadh smiled a frail smile. Her greenish pallor was almost transparent. She drew a shaky breath and began to speak quietly and slowly.

'It is a great privilege for me to address you all . . .' There were loud cheers from some over-enthusiastic members of the merrow clan. The old empress smiled.

'Looking out at you all, I see so many different clans, families, committees and tribes. I see the merrow there!' More loud cheers! 'The murdhvagh, the mermen, the huire, the merrminnen, the havfrue, the ceasg, the sirens. I would also like to extend my deepest gratitude to all the other sea folk who share this watery world alongside us: the whales, dolphins, turtles, seals, sharks . . . the eleven thousand species of fish, and to all the other forms of life too numerous to mention.

'There is also my dear friend and travel companion from the northern seas, Leviathan, the blue whale. He came to bring me the sad news of my sister's passing which he had heard from a white-sided dolphin from this area.'

Emerald knew that must be Wavesweeper, her mother's pet dolphin.

'Without hesitation, Leviathan offered to bring me from the Sea of Cortez, where I was visiting with the cardon clan. The Cardons had asked me to come and give my blessing over the birth of twin mermaids. It was the first birth for many a year. Joy and sorrow all in the one day,' she smiled sadly.

'Well, the blue whale brought me safely to your shores, despite considerable danger from whaling ships and the long-line drift nets that stretch a curtain of death as far as the eye can see. But more of that horrible subject later.

Last but not least to my relations of the Emerald Isle, especially dearest Pearl, Tarmon and all their family.'

Loud applause and cheering. Azure elbowed Jade, who in turn pushed Emerald, nearly knocking her off her position on the pillar. Emerald shrieked. Her mother looked up at her and placed a finger on her lips. There was no mistaking what she meant. The three sisters settled back quietly.

'I'm sorry I was not here for the funeral of my dear sister Murgen. It seems it all happened quite suddenly. As I said, I was visiting the cardon clan in the Sea of Cortez. Well here I am, and glad to be with you all again.'

Despite the quietly spoken voice of the old empress, her words seemed to echo around the caverns, chambers, tunnels and alcoves of the palace. Then in a deadly serious tone she said: 'Have you ever looked down into darkness, into a place where even imagination has not entered? I have, and I know my dear sister did too.

'In the great silence a voice may be heard or felt. It's like a voice you cannot begin to imagine, but its sound can sustain you. Is it the voice of the sea or the universe? I don't really know. When you have heard that beautiful voice in joy, your heart is filled with the greatest of ecstasy, for it is the voice of bliss. But when you hear that voice in sorrow, your heart is sent to the core of sadness. The voice has been sounded and now it's the voice of grief.

'The world, my dear children, is at the edge between light and darkness. When the world was sent out to us we were the custodians of this travelling planet. Over seventy percent of its surface was our liquid world. The nusham were given the rest, along with the land and air creatures. Now, because of the foolishness and selfishness of the nusham, we have slipped off the shelf of light into darkness.'

'Death to the nusham!' a merman shouted.

'Destroy the evil doers!' shouted another.

'Let us attack them and drown every last one of them and let coral grow over their dead bones,' yelled a third.

'No, dear friends,' said the old empress. 'There is already too much violence in the world. We must replace darkness with light, bring wisdom where there is only ignorance. Now I know some of you have to use violence to catch a meal or defend your territory; I'm not condemning you, as you conform to the natural law. But I do condemn the violence of power, pleasure and greed that is practised by the nusham.'

The old mermaid rested back in the throne. Pearl offered the old woman some fruit and a drink of unsalted water.

'Thank you, my dear.'

'Would anyone like to speak while the empress partakes of a little refreshment?' enquired Pearl.

'I am Zaka from Chesapeake Bay in Maryland. I have seen the bay slowly destroyed by nusham industrial waste.'

Another merman raised his voice: 'I am Zolta. Where I live,

the Aral Sea in Uzbekistan, is in the throes of death.'

Others had similar horror stories. Some — the havfrue, the meerweiber and meerminnen — told of what was happening to rivers, wetlands, estuaries, lakes and ponds. The poisoning, the dredging, the damming, the draining. A suire spoke about the pollution of the atmosphere by what is called carbon dioxide. An old mermaid shouted out that if the nusham have evil in their hearts they would be destroyed by their own actions. There was loud applause.

'The mighty sea lies stricken,' said another with a great sigh.

'The nusham want to take the spirit out of the sea and leave us with a grey corpse,' shouted an old murdhvagh merman.

'I hear your words,' the old empress began again. 'And they are all true. We know the hardest journey to make in life can sometimes be from one heart to another. Although I have never had any personal contact with the nusham I am prepared to believe that they are not evil. Ignorant yes, but not truly evil. I have seen them from a distance, playing on the beaches, I have listened to their laughter, and watched them enjoying venturing into the water. Their children look like any one of our own children, innocent and pure. Of course without the tail and the webbed fingers,' she added brightly. There was gentle laughter from some of the listeners.

Her tone changed again as she spoke.

'We have thought long and hard about this and I know our mermaid laws have forbidden us to have any dealings with the nusham. But times are changing. The old laws were useful for their time but we are now in an era of great calamity. We need to go beyond the laws to get to the heart of the matter. For that reason we are asking a number of mermen and mermaids to give up their marine way of life and become as nusham.'

Shock waves passed through the entire gathering.

'This is against tradition,' shouted a merman with a long white flowing beard.

'I am aware of this,' said the empress.

'You cannot go against tradition,' he shouted forcefully.

A few more voiced their agreement with the merman.

'Without a future we will have no past,' said the empress. 'It was our tradition in the siren days to lure fisher nusham to their death by drowning. I am glad we have abandoned that barbaric practice. Remember that not all tradition is good and worth preserving. We must evolve or die out, that is the choice we are faced with.

'Tomorrow we will be performing the ceremony of transformation. There is already one among us who has been selected by my late sister.'

Pearl's mother looked at Emerald and so did her sisters. They broke out into uncontrollable crying and wailing.

The old empress looked up at the three young girls. She beckoned down the one who was to go through the ritual of transformation. Emerald's sisters pulled at her arms trying to prevent her from moving but she freed herself and swam down slowly and silently to be alongside the old empress. There was a look of shock and sadness on the faces of her friends Dorad, Lutra and Grypus as they watched.

Emerald smiled a sad smile at the old empress. Moruadh placed her leafy hands on Emerald's face.

'You are the one?'

'Yes,' said Emerald.

'Are you afraid?' she asked in whispered tones.

'I am terribly afraid. But if my grandmother and you want me to go to them, I will.'

'There have been very few volunteers,' said Moruadh. 'Some of the mermen have been ordered to go, but you are willing?'

'Yes,' said Emerald.

'Well, may the great spirit bless you.' With that she kissed Emerald on the forehead.

'This is my daughter, Emerald,' said Pearl to the congregation. 'She has been chosen to make the journey to the land people, the nusham. She has welcomed the challenge and if anyone can succeed I know it is my dear daughter.' She embraced Emerald. Emerald felt a warmth from her mother that she had not felt since she was a small child.

Her father, too, made a big gesture then hugged her tightly. The crowds cheered. Some wept at the thought of the dangers facing one so young.

'Speech!' one shouted up, then another. Soon all were cheering and shouting: 'Speech!'

Emerald was terrified at the idea of addressing so many of her kind. Her tail felt like jelly.

'Go on, my child,' Pearl coaxed her.

Emerald stood awkwardly, her tail trembling uncontrollably.

'I . . . I . . . I have been given a great honour and a great challenge . . .' Loud applause. 'Grandmother Nature, as she was affectionately known, said to us that she could hear the sea suffering. I could not begin to imagine that depth of feeling or understanding. All I know is that I loved her dearly, as indeed I love you all, especially my parents, my sisters and dear Moruadh, whose words struck so deeply into our minds and hearts. I am no heroine, but I too love my home, the sea. It has been like a mother to us all.

'To swim in an orchard of soft white coral. To awake to a sun-filled sea. To float lazily on the surface of the water watching the heavenly stars. To watch a full moon rise above the dark water and burnish the waves with her silvery light. To swim with my sisters and frolic with dear Dorad. All these things are so precious to me as a mermaid. I don't want to lose any of them, but I know that somehow I must walk the dry road with the nusham. I must try to understand them and try to help them to understand our ways, the ways of the sea people.' She paused. 'That's all I have to say. Thank you.'

The crowds cheered and clapped. The mammals and fish thrashed the water with great excitement and joy.

'Well done, my child,' said Pearl. 'Your grandmother schooled you well.'

Tarmon, her father, patted her on the back, then he spoke a few words:

'I thank dear Moruadh, the empress, for her words of great wisdom. I, too, thank my daughter Emerald for her courage, impressive in one so young. I thank you all for making the journey here. It is very much appreciated. And we thank you for your support and understanding.

'And now to the celebrations. We can offer the finest singers and musicians the sea people can produce. There are refreshments for all and sleeping accommodation for those requiring it.' There was loud applause and cheering. Tarmon raised his right hand to silence them. 'Tomorrow at first light there will be the ceremony of transformation. This secret ritual you can bring away with you, to perform in your own good time on your mermen, mermaids and sea-maidens. Tomorrow you may witness the ceremony on our dear daughter Emerald.'

As everyone started to move to the banquet area, Azure and Jade swam down and grabbed hold of Emerald.

'Dear sister, how could you agree to this?' snapped Azure.

'You are being very foolish,' said Jade. 'Do you realise what you are letting yourself in for?'

'The nusham are a horde of killers,' said Azure. 'Everyone knows that.'

'Cop on!' said Jade, shaking Emerald by the shoulders. 'You are letting yourself be seduced by the old empress's words. It's all right for her, she's old. She doesn't have to metamorphose into some alien being with the blood of every creature upon its hands.'

'No, I can't believe it,' cried Emerald. 'We need to know, we need to understand.'

'We do understand, we do know,' retorted Jade. 'It is the land people who don't know or care.'

'I must go,' insisted Emerald. 'I promised.'

'You promised! I can't see what a blind bit of good it would do to have a naïve sixteen-year-old mermaid going to live with the nusham.'

'There are others,' insisted Emerald.

'Yes, many mermen with more brawn than brain,' Azure flared. 'Most of them spend more time flexing their muscles and riding the giant waves, than taking the least bit of notice of what's happening to the world's oceans. Oh, they'll grumble about a discarded fishing net or noisy nusham activity in the water. But that's about the sum total of it.'

'Talk to mother later when she's relaxed,' said Jade. 'Explain that you agreed without thinking, and that you were flattered by being chosen.' Then on reflection she said: 'No, better tell father, he will be more understanding.'

'Besides, you're his favourite,' they teased. 'So let's all go into the banqueting hall together and we'll call father and explain all.'

The three sisters moved towards the great hall where the merriment had begun. There was a beautiful chorus of singing as the suire sang old sea songs. Emerald looked at her mother and father. They were smiling and laughing along with the elders and the different visitors. She had a pain in her stomach with tension. Her sisters were steering her towards her parents. People applauded Emerald as she passed by.

The young mermaid desperately wanted to commune with her wild friends, Dorad, Lutra and Grypus.

'They have left,' said a deep voice from behind. It was the orca. He must have read her mind.

'Why?' she asked anxiously.

'They didn't say, they just slipped away.'

'Leave me,' said Emerald, freeing her arms from the grip of her sisters.

'Listen,' said Azure. 'If they insist on one of our clan going it will be Jade or me, we are both older than you.'

'I'm not going,' said Jade anxiously.

'Well, I will if I have to,' said Azure. 'I'll bring the dagger I found in that old Spanish shipwreck. If those nusham try to abuse me, I'll kill myself.'

'No!' Emerald said. There was panic in her voice. 'I don't want you going either, no way! Listen, I need to be alone for a time. I won't say yes or no until I have time to think it through.'

'We understand,' they said in unison.

Emerald threw her arms around both of them, pulling them tightly to her body. She kissed them and tears streamed down their faces.

'Here we are, crying again,' she laughed through the tears. 'I couldn't have better sisters than you two. No matter what happens, I love you dearly.'

Azure pulled away. 'Why don't you go for a moonlight swim. It will help to clear your head.'

'Think carefully over your decisions and whatever you decide we will back you one hundred per cent,' added Jade.

They hugged again and Emerald slipped away, but not before thanking the orca.

'I did nothing,' he replied. 'But if you should ever need me you know how to call a dolphin, I'm sure.'

She rubbed her hand along his mouth. He opened it slightly and she rubbed his gums and tongue. She knew dolphins and whales liked that. Then she slipped out of the palace without anyone taking any notice.

Chapter 8

The night was cold. Heavy black clouds veiled the stars. Emerald moved silently in the dark waters. There was a brooding silence as if the sea had taken on her mood. 'Where was Dorad?' she wondered. 'Had Lutra gone with Grypus back to his island?' She really needed to know what they felt about her decision. She had been so sure she was doing the right thing, journeying to the realm of the nusham. Especially since her grandmother on her deathbed had picked her. But her sisters' words and warnings had now upset and confused her.

Her mother seemed to think it was right to take part in the transformation ceremony and leave. Was it because now she could say to the elders and the others of the clan: 'My daughter was chosen and she agreed without hesitation?' A daughter of hers would naturally rise to the challenge, and risk her life for the greater glory of all. Emerald's thoughts troubled her even more now that she was on her own. She started to kick the water, preferring the sound of splashing water and hoping it would drown out her thoughts.

Then when she tired of that, her body dipped below the curtain of the surface into the realms of the night world. She closed her eyes and moved through the water as silently as the currents. Where was the comfort and security she needed so much from her family and friends? Had they all deserted her in her hour of need? She opened her eyes. They quickly became accustomed to the darkness. On she swam through the nocturnal hours. Sometimes she would glimpse silvery skins of fish as shoals flared across her path. Below her a blue shark appeared, then vanished into the gloom.

She was still troubled with the feeling of being alone, isolated and separated from all she cared about. Looking to the surface she could see the silver orb of the moon reflecting on the skin of the water. She hurried to the surface. The heavy clouds had passed and the night belonged to the moon and the stars. The very sight cheered her somewhat. Then a sleek smooth shape brushed her back.

'Dorad!' she exclaimed. 'I thought you had abandoned me. Let me give you a hug.'

The dolphin bobbed up and down, splashing the surface with his flippers. He moved his head playfully to the side. She hugged him and whispered how good it was to have him by her, especially tonight of all nights.

'You were told to keep away from me tonight, but why?' Emerald wondered. 'My mother said I should be on my own, so I could prepare myself. But I can't bear to be alone tonight. I'm glad you didn't obey!'

A wave seemed to scoop her up. She turned only to see the big face of Grypus appearing, it seemed, from nowhere. Then Lutra arrived from below the dark waters.

'Oh,' she smiled. 'I wish I was an octopus. I would be able to embrace you all at the same time.'

'We like you just the way you are,' said the turtle.

'Let's go and talk, and just be together, dear friends. Let's go to the lonely cave near the lighthouse. There we can sit and listen to the sound of the breakers.' Emerald climbed onto Dorad's back and the others followed as they made their way to the rocky shore.

Emerald closed her eyes and let the sound of the waves and wind penetrate every part of her body. Her fears began to subside. She felt invigorated again and knew it was because of the arrival of her dear companions. Passing near the sheer cliffs that were being buffeted by the waves below, Emerald saw a wonderful sight.

'Stop a moment,' she commanded Dorad. Grypus' and Lutra's head bobbed up from the churning surface. Watching from a secret vantage point they saw small shapes emerge from the carved and scarred cliff faces. Jostling bands of adult guillemots watched anxiously from the swelling waves below as their fledglings prepared to make their first leap into the watery world. Unable to fly, the young needed coaxing to make their dramatic leap into the unknown. They could not risk it by day, for marauding great black-backed gulls and herring gulls would soon make an easy meal of them.

Then it began. The young birds started to leap from the safety of the cliffs into the swell. Gliding, free falling, fluttering down to the sea, they all made it, hurrying after their parents to the safety of the open sea.

'Isn't that so special?' said Emerald. The others agreed.

Grypus admitted he had not seen it before, or if he had, he certainly had not taken any notice of it. Now that he had observed it he was glad to witness the fledgelings succeeding in such a dangerous hurdle of their young life.

Emerald felt Dorad move from under her. She nearly lost her grip on his dorsal fin.

'Hey, what's up?' she called, as the dolphin sped over the breaking waves to where water pulsed and tunnelled through a cave which later became a blowhole.

'Wow, this is lovely,' said Emerald, as she entered the large cave. She pulled herself onto some boulders.

Grypus and Lutra followed. The old seal seemed a bit jumpy, looking over his shoulders frequently. Emerald enquired as to what was the matter. It appeared that it was a very long time since he had even alighted on the larger island where the nusham lived. He had spent most of his latter years on his own island, fishing nearby. He didn't feel too comfortable about being this close.

'Relax,' said Lutra. 'Sure, many a seal colony spends a great deal of time on this big island.'

'Well good luck to them. I am happy and contented on my own island.'

'Oh, I'm sorry for bringing you so far away from your place,' said Emerald.

'It's all right,' snorted Grypus. 'I just like to keep vigilant. You can't be too careful.'

'There's no one to be seen around here,' said Emerald. 'I've come several times at night to these quiet shores. I did see one nusham several times. He walks the beach, picking up bits of driftwood.'

'One too many,' retorted Grypus. 'Now, since we've come here perhaps you might sing another one of your lovely mermaid songs?'

Dorad nodded in agreement. Emerald began to sing. Her lovely clear voice echoed around the cave. The wind seemed to carry the sound up along the cliffs then out to sea. Emerald could see her friends were becoming melancholy.

'Oh please don't be sad. I need you all to be pleased for me, and with my decision. I am excited and terrified. I feel duty bound to take on this mission and yet I ask: 'Why me, why not someone older and wiser.'

'Dear Emerald, we are sad that you have to go on this journey to the nusham world,' said Lutra. 'And maybe it is selfish of us, but we don't want to lose you. We have only recently really got to know you and tomorrow you will be gone from us.'

Tears streamed down her face. 'You will always be with me in my heart.'

'Your mother asked us not to visit with you tonight,' said Grypus. 'But we had to. We cannot come to the ceremony tomorrow; it will be too painful. Our only fear is that if you go you will not come back.'

'I will,' she cried, 'once I talk to the nusham and explain what is happening to our world because of their exploitation. As soon as they understand I will return and we can all be together again. And I will sing to you every day and massage your aches and . . .'

'Suppose they change you to their way of thinking?' interrupted Grypus. 'Suppose they not only have you looking like a nusham but thinking like one?'

'What do you mean? I will never think like them, never!' Emerald rocked back and forth, crying loudly.

'Dear, dear child, I'm sorry,' said Grypus. 'I didn't mean to say such a foolish thing. Please excuse an old fool who speaks without thinking.'

'No, you are right. I could change. They might have some magic power over me that could do it. But I will try to resist it with all my being.' There was a long silence. Emerald recovered and said with a sad smile: 'Let's hope the first nusham I encounter will be friendly.'

Dorad splashed the water with his tail. 'What is it?' Emerald asked, seeing that the dolphin was either excited or agitated. Dorad had remembered once overhearing Murgen, Emerald's grandmother, telling a story to the elders. Apparently she had an encounter with a nusham, a long, long time ago and she arranged the contact by leaving something of hers on the seashore. The nusham that found it would be the one with whom the contact would be made.

Emerald immediately thought of the old man with the silver beard who walked the beach collecting driftwood. If her first encounter with a nusham could be with someone like him it would not seem too scary a proposition for her.

She thought about it for a moment. Then pulling a comb from her hair she asked: 'Will this do?' She held out the beautiful jewel-studded comb. Dorad nodded. 'Will you please take it up to the sandy beach and place it near the shoreline?'

Dorad clicked and opened his beak. Emerald tossed the comb at him. Catching it between his teeth, he quickly turned and plunged, diving under the water. As quick as a flash he was out of the blowhole heading up along the cliffs, past the lighthouse and on to the quiet beach. Allowing the waves to wash him up onto the beach, Dorad dropped the comb near some dry seaweed.

The eerie choking call of the manx shearwater flying over the sea startled the dolphin. Quickly he slipped back into the safety of the water. Under the cover of darkness he had achieved the task for lovely Emerald. Quickly propelling himself in the water he returned to the others.

'Thank you, dear Dorad,' said Emerald, giving him a hug.

'Well, my child,' said Lutra. 'You have cast your fate upon the wind, as the old saying goes.'

'Listen, there's no reason why I can't still see you all when I'm living on the land, is there?'

'No reason,' said Dorad.

'But you must be discreet,' said Lutra. 'You don't want to attract unwelcome attention. It could put us all in danger. '

'I think it's time for one more song,' said Emerald, feeling a lot happier and calmer. Again the young mermaid regaled her friends with her beautiful singing voice and a charming song. 'If anyone can work the magic on the nusham, it's you!' said Lutra.

Emerald smiled. 'I sincerely hope so.'

'Look,' said Grypus. Outside the cave and over the horizon the grey light of dawn could be seen.

Emerald took a deep breath. 'I must go now,' she said. She smiled the saddest of smiles, as tears ran freely down her cheeks.

Chapter 9

A solemn procession of mermaids and mermen filed past Emerald. She stood trembling, flanked by her sisters, Azure and Jade. Some of the mermaids broke file to give Emerald an embrace, others shook her hand warmly. The music being played by the mermen on their musical instruments was melancholy in its tones. Pearl and Tarmon appeared on a chariot pulled by a pod of common dolphins.

Then the blue whale arrived slowly bearing Moruadh astride the great whale, with sea maidens on either side of her. Emerald's sisters were silent. They respected her decision to go through with the service of transformation. They squeezed her hands tightly in a supportive way, but kept their gaze fixed straight ahead as the different sea people got into position near the ceremonial stones that stood beyond the palace walls.

Pearl moved slowly over to Emerald and cupped her hands around her daughter's face. They locked eyes together.

'Are you ready, my child?' she asked tenderly. Emerald nodded. Her mother slowly removed her hands from Emerald's face. 'It's a pity we've never had much talk together. Life is too busy for us adults. Still, your grandmother was always there for you.'

'Not anymore,' said Emerald.

'True, child.' Pearl looked at her other daughters. 'Thank you, my children, for being so supportive of each other.'

Their father, Tarmon, came over and joined his family. 'All set?' he enquired. Emerald smiled nervously. 'You will be missed so much around here. The choir mistress says you will be a terrible loss to the choir.'

Emerald smiled. 'Sure, Azure's and Jade's voices are the finest in the realm. They are gifted with such sweet melodious voices they can enchant even the wind and the sea.'

Her father smiled awkwardly. 'What I was trying to say, dearest Emerald, is that we will all miss you. But what you, and the others who make the journey to the different lands, do, is a very courageous deed . . .'

'A matter of life and death,' added Pearl. 'But you know that.'

'I do,' said Emerald.

Tarmon pulled her to him in a strong embrace.

'Here she comes.' Voices whispered among the crowds of watchers. The blue whale moved slowly and silently near the ceremonial stone. Moruadh beckoned to two mermen. All eyes watched as from one of the many tunnels below the palace the mermen appeared holding a metre chest. They brought it over to the empress and lifted up the lid. They then removed what looked like a long blanket, which they held up. The old mermaid stroked her hand along the centre of the sheet. It was made from different seaweeds: kelp, knotted bladder, spiral, toothed and channelled wracks. Moruadh nodded approvingly.

'Good morning, citizens of the sea. We are gathered together on this very joyful and sad occasion. Joyful in so far as our dear child Emerald is about to make the most important journey of her life on our behalf. And sad that we should have to sever her from her family and loved ones. For one so young she has shown great courage and I know she will have your prayers and good thoughts wherever she finds herself. There is always loss in choice. If you choose to be a nusham, you lose the life of a mermaid. If you stay a mermaid, you lose the chance of a privileged glimpse of another world and serving the sea people in such a vital way.'

Distant thunder could be heard from the north east. The sky and water seemed to take on an eerie gloom. Turning back to the blanket of seaweed and gesturing to it she continued:

'What these two handsome mermen are holding up is the garment of transformation. All last night the suires collected the tufts of seaweed from the four intertidal zones, and the kelp from the forest. Then, they wove this blanket while I recited the magic words over the seaweed. Its fronds, crust, thallus, stipe, leaves and holdfast carry the secret words.

'This ceremony will be performed by the elders from the different tribes and clans over the coming weeks. Today, I am privileged to conduct the ceremony on dear Emerald.' She waved her hand indicating she wanted Emerald beside her. Emerald looked at her sisters, then hurried over to the empress and bowed gracefully, kissing the old mermaid's hand. The empress pulled her closer and moved her face near to Emerald's.

'Are you sure you want to continue with the ceremony?' she whispered. 'No one will think any less of you if you decline to go. There are three others who have offered to take your place.'

'No. I'm ready as I ever will be,' declared Emerald.

The old empress turned to the crowd. Her voice seemed strong and powerful.

'The nusham have lost their relationship with the rest of creation. They have displaced themselves from nature. They want to dominate, master, possess and exploit. They must be taught that they have created an artificial, mechanised world, a world where they seek to impose their laws over the rest of life. The message we must bring to the nusham is that they belong to the natural world, and not, as they seem to believe, that the world belongs to them. Their actions so far have only brought disorder in nature and among their own kind. They must be made aware, and forced to acknowledge their extreme forms of cruelty in their crimes against nature and wild folk.'

The empress began to look tired and frail. Emerald linked her arm. The old mermaid kept her composure. 'Let the ceremony begin,' she commanded.

'I wish I had your words,' Emerald whispered.

'The words will come to you, my child,' the empress answered.

The choir began to sing a lament. The horns blew in accompaniment to the singing. The sound of the sea grew louder.

The old empress turned and began to whisper words over Emerald's head. It was the ancient mermaid language that Emerald had heard Murgen speak on special occasions, but she did not know what the words meant.

The blanket was brought closer to Emerald. Her stomach tightened.

'Our people must remain a secret, a myth to the nusham. For if they know about us they will hunt us down, the way they do the whales.'

A drum sounded.

'Good luck my child. May the spirit be with you.' The empress kissed Emerald on the forehead and smiled sadly. The mermen began to wind the blanket around Emerald. The touch of it gave her goosebumps. It felt slimy and slippery. In a wide clockwise movement they wrapped the olive-brown blanket around her body. Emerald felt a sense of panic, verging on claustrophobia, as it wrapped around her face. She wanted to scream but remained silent. There were muffled voices to be heard. It sounded like distant wailing. The blanket tightened around her body. It seemed to take on her shape. Emerald felt faint. There were loud cries of gulls; they seemed to be screaming in her brain. She began to lose consciousness.

There was a deep silence. The onlookers gazed on the shrouded body of the young mermaid as she was laid horizontally along the back of the blue whale. The chorus of voices started up again as the Moruadh kissed Pearl on each cheek, then shook Tarmon's hand. She was helped on to the whale who turned to head out into the vastness of the ocean.

The others began to disband — mermen, mermaids, suire, merrow, sea-maidens, meerminnen, morhan, groach vor, marmaeler, havfrue, meerweiber, mara-warra. Kelpies, daoine mara, havmand, nökke, söedouen, näcken, neckers, all began to depart for their homeward journey. They embraced the Emerald clan to thank them for their hospitality and then began to leave silently and slowly.

Tears flowed freely from the mermaids and the mermen of the Emerald city as they watched the blue whale move out over the waves carrying their beloved Emerald and the empress Moruadh. They knew somewhere in the 'middle open sea' the young mermaid would be let go to float in the gloomy silent waters where no plants grow and the sun did not penetrate. That is where the transformation would take place.

Chapter 10

Jimmy Talbot looked seawards through the window of his house. He could see bad weather was blowing in across the sea. By his calculations he reckoned he could get a walk in before it turned nasty. Grabbing his cap, he pulled on his jacket. Emptying the last of his tea from his mug, he placed the mug, along with his breakfast plate, into the sink. He would wash them later; he'd better, he thought to himself, the dirty dishes were piling up.

He felt in his pocket for his glasses, then for his keys. He had both, not that he needed his glasses except for reading. He was becoming more long-sighted which was okay with him. At sixty-eight years of age, he couldn't complain.

He always gave a look towards the lighthouse as he left his house. He had enjoyed his life as a lighthouse keeper. It was tough at times, indeed even with moments of sheer terror. But for most of the time it was without too much excitement. Some of the younger men found it boring at times, but not Jimmy Talbot. There was always the sea and the sky. Forever changing. Beautiful on a calm day. Exciting and scary on a bad, stormy one.

His friends nick-named him 'Sparrow', because he would leave food out for the birds, especially the migrant ones. To some people, all birds looked the same, but not so to Jimmy. He remembered seeing the snow buntings one year and on another occasion rescuing a very bedraggled rough-legged buzzard. He had lots of good memories of his time as a lighthouse keeper.

He kept notes of the different ships that passed by the

lighthouse, of the wrecks and the rescues. He recorded the sea creatures he'd seen, the dolphins, the porpoises, the seals, several basking sharks and some pilot whales. And once he sighted a great white shark, but there was no one to verify it except himself.

Now it was all automation with the lighthouses, and their keepers were no longer needed. He was glad of the chance to buy the house beside the lighthouse, having spent over forty years working there. Making his way down the steep steps he headed for the beach. It was a beautiful place. Very few people walked the beach or swam there. It was as if the cliffs, the lighthouse, and the beach belonged to him. He carried an old hazel stick which he used to probe and check the rotting seaweed for any sea beans that may have drifted in on the tide. It was a lonely quiet stretch of beach.

As he strolled along the wide golden sand he saw a kestrel hunting across the sand dunes in search of insects or small rodents. He watched as it rode the gentle sea breeze and moved in leisurely flight. Jimmy noted it down in his little book, then scolded himself for forgetting to bring binoculars. He enjoyed the life of a beachcomber. You could never tell what might be washed ashore, especially near the cliffs. He had found an old army helmet once and a barometer. The barometer case was guitar-shaped and made of oak, with a lovely carving of the Cutty Sark. When he cleaned and polished it up it looked marvellous. Of course the barometer itself was damaged and he replaced it with a new one. It now hung proudly in the hallway of his house. A gift from the sea.

He had collected so much driftwood that he had many a good fire from it. He used some of the wood for carving. He carved mainly seabirds. People who came to visit would admire

them, and he usually sent them home with one under their arm. It gave him pleasure carving them and if people got pleasure from admiring them that was good enough reward for him. His nephew, Chris, had a number of his pieces: the dolphin, the gannet and the seal. They were his finest pieces; he'd spent a lot of time carving them.

Suddenly Jimmy's eye caught sight of a fulmar out at sea. There was no mistaking its stiff-winged gliding and weaving above the waves. He laughed when he remembered as a youngster peeking over a cliff to see a fulmar sitting on a ledge . . . he was so close he could nearly touch it. He wondered if it was sitting on an egg or hiding a chick. Unfortunately when he reached his hand down to try to shift the adult bird to get a better view he got more than he bargained for. The fulmar, in defence of its young chick, spat from its mouth a smelly oily fluid from its stomach.

Well, he was in a sorry state going home that day. His father scolded him for going up to the cliffs on his own. Jimmy explained, as only a ten-year-old could, that the bird was a rare species and worth climing the cliffs. 'You'll be a rare species if you ever come back smelling like that again,' his mother had warned as she looked at his clothes. 'These are only fit for burning.' After that Jimmy never allowed himself to get too close to the 'tube noses' again.

Now the fulmars are a common sight around the island.

Up ahead Jimmy spotted a fine piece of driftwood lying along the shoreline. As he got closer he could see the holes — long channels in the wood — made by the ship worms. Still, it would burn well when the winter gales blew. Nearby a shore crab scurried for cover in among the seaweed as the shadow of the old man passed over it. Jimmy could see what the crab had been feeding on, a dead dogfish.

Lifting up the piece of driftwood he examined it. It was a post, probably from the porch of someone's house. He wondered where. It didn't feel too heavy, he reckoned he could carry it on the way back.

Then his eye caught sight of something sparkling in the brief sunshine that pierced through the clouds. Dropping the wood he bent down and picked up the object. He couldn't believe his eyes. It was a beautiful comb, full of pearls and sapphires. Pulling out his handkerchief he began to dust off the sand. He had never found anything as beautiful as this. If it wasn't some kind of costume jewellery he reckoned it must be very valuable. He would show it to his nephew. Chris would be able to find out whether it was costume jewellery or the real thing. Either way, it was beautiful to look at. He carefully wrapped it in his handkerchief and put it in his pocket, very pleased with his unusual find.

Chapter 11

Emerald awoke dazed and confused. She was floating on her back on the surface of the water. The waves buffeted her body as she was carried up the peaks and down the valleys of the dark green waves. She felt very strange, as if she'd been awakened suddenly from a beautiful dream.

She had been dreaming, dreaming with the sea, sharing its thoughts, its joys and fears. Wondrous creatures from the sea floor swam by, then she could see her Grandmother Nature, dearest Murgen. 'Do not be afraid, my child,' she whispered softly in Emerald's ear, while her hands began to remove the seaweed blanket from her body.

Murgen looked iridescent and younger but it was her. Emerald reached to embrace her and nestle in her gentle arms,

but all she clasped was water. She felt like a creature leaving a cocoon and being metamorphosed. There was a tingling sensation in her body. It was more than the feeling of wave-splashed water on her skin.

She was almost afraid to look at the lower part of her body. With trembling hands she reached down along her body, exploring it. The scales were gone, soft skin replaced them. She could feel goosebumps as her body trembled. Then braving it she looked down and saw the body of a nusham. She could hardly believe her eyes. But it had happened. She had become a land person!

She knew now there was no going home. She felt so alone moving among the lonely waves in the vast expanse of water. The winds were blowing strong plumes of spray skywards from the tips of the waves. There was a storm brewing; she could sense it. The winds agitated the seas. She felt herself being thrust upwards, then dropped down, being tossed from side to side. The sky darkened and the sea seemed to run wild. Strong currents pulled her body in every direction. The sea began to hiss. Overhead heavy black clouds hovered, like a predator ready to pounce.

Then the deafening sound of rolling thunder panicked her. She turned on her stomach and began to swim; her eyes were stinging from the seaspray. As she weaved in and out among the walls of sea more thunder sounded. It seemed closer. The water surged even higher. She moved among the frantic waves. There was another roll of thunder, followed by a flash of lightning that ripped across the sky and stabbed the distant horizon. There was no sign of any wild folk; none of her family or friends to comfort her. Yet Emerald knew this was how it must be.

She had been told by the old empress that after a year, during the winter solstices, she could return to her people. She could also be ordered by the elders if there was an emergency. That seemed unlikely. A year seemed an eternity away, but at least there was hope that she could return home to her kin. She would carry that hope through the long days and nights ahead. The sky opened and a torrent of rain began.

*   *   *

The rain lashed at the window panes and the window frame rattled. Jimmy Talbot sat in the comfort of his home, grateful that he wasn't out on such a stormy night. He hoped that any seafarer out at sea would reach port safely.

Putting down his book on the life of Captain Cooke, he began to make himself a little supper of toast and cheese, and the essential pot of tea. He was glad he had lit a fire earlier. It wasn't very good weather for summer. Well, nearly autumn, he corrected himself. He checked the time on the mantelpiece clock. Nine thirty, he had missed the news on the television. Probably all bad news as usual.

While the bread was toasting he changed the record on the record player. Some Maria Callas would be nice after Enrico Caruso to keep the sound of the storm out. Nothing pleased him better than reading, and listening to old records. He smiled and mused at the thought of his nephew telling him to update his system. 'You can get all that stuff on pure CD sound instead of listening to all that crackling noise.' Jimmy would always retort with a remark that the ritual of removing the record from the sleeve, the cleaning of the vinyl and the needle, the way one held the record without putting fingerprints on it, was all part of the pleasure.

He sat down again to read his book, with his tray of supper beside him and the sound of Maria Callas singing. His eyes fell on the beautiful comb he had found earlier. Picking it up he studied it again; he could not get over the lovely delicate work. Then placing it back on a shelf, he tucked into his supper. The clock sounded midnight. He awoke with a start. He had fallen asleep beside the warm fire. The needle of the record player was stuck in a groove near the end of the record. It made a repeating sound.

As he got up from the chair to free the needle he thought he saw a shadowy form pass by the kitchen window. Nobody would be calling at this hour, in fact he rarely had visitors. Maybe it was just his imagination. He stopped the record player, put the record back in its sleeve and gave a big yawn. Time for bed, he told himself. The rain was still beating against the window panes and the wind sighed around the house.

He went into his bedroom to put on the bedside light, then returned to the sitting room to turn off the lights. The fire was still lighting but would burn itself out. He put the fireguard to it, then took up his book that had fallen to the floor. As he flicked the pages trying to remember what page he was at, he heard a sound outside the kitchen door. It was a gentle tapping, almost like a bird flapping. Was he dreaming or what? Maybe it was a seabird blown in from the storm, he mused. It wouldn't be the first time. After all the cliffs were still full of bird colonies.

There was a definite rapping on the door; it was louder this time. He began to feel a bit nervous. As he moved closer he thought he heard sobbing. Lightning flashed, illuminating the darkened kitchen. There was someone outside his kitchen door; he saw the shape framed by the lightning.

'Who's there?' he called sharply.

There was no answer, only more knocking. There was a sense of urgency about it. Perhaps it was somebody stranded, caught out by the storm. They might need help. What was he doing hesitating?

He opened the door wide. A figure loomed out of the darkness. To his amazement, a young naked girl stood trembling on the step. She stood pale and ghost-like. Her hair was matted to her face as the rain and wind lashed her body.

'Come in, child,' he commanded. 'You'll get your death of cold out there.'

Emerald ran into the darkened room, brightened only by the dying fire. She huddled in the farthest corner. He quickly bolted the kitchen door and entered the sitting room. He could just make out her shape hiding in the shadows. Her eyes shone like cats' eyes from the flickering fire. She sat huddled, clutching her body. She looked like a frightened hare.

The old man gingerly reached over and put on his reading light. She jerked and turned inwards, pulling herself towards the safety of the corner of the room.

'Don't be afraid, young lady. You're safe. No one is going to hurt you.'

Silence.

'Are you alone? Were you swimming on a night like this? Do you live near by?'

Silence.

He went over to the fire and began to stoke it, then he placed some briquettes on the red remains. Emerald watched as the flames and sparks licked up the chimney. The man put down the poker.

'My name is Jimmy Talbot, what's yours?'

Silence.

'Can you talk? Listen, I'll make a nice hot drink of chocolate that will warm you.'

He hurried into the kitchen and fumbled about looking for the chocolate and a mug. Emerald just stayed in the corner clutching at her nakedness.

He arrived back in with a mug of hot chocolate and some biscuits.

'Here you are, young lady. I'll leave them on the table here.'

He went into the bathroom and took out a bath towel. He went slowly over to her and dropped it over her back. She jerked nervously.

'Listen, young lady. I'll leave you to your supper. There are two bedrooms upstairs. Or if you want to stay down here and sleep on the sofa, that's fine with me. Make yourself at home and don't forget to drink your chocolate. You're safe here, don't fret!' He paused. 'I'm off to bed now, so we can talk in the morning. Goodnight and God bless.' He went into his bedroom and closed the door.

Emerald didn't move but listened anxiously. She had made it this far and was in the home of one of the nusham. The room felt so warm and cosy. She pulled the towel around her. It felt good on the skin. She saw the light go off under the door of the nusham's bedroom. A few moments later she got to her feet and walked around the room. The sofa felt soft to the touch, so did the armchair. The aroma of the milky chocolate filled her nostrils. It smelled nice. She moved over to the fire, the heat felt wonderful after what she had been through. As a mermaid the cold weather never bothered her, but now she was glad of the heat.

She marvelled at the beauty of the yellow licks of flame dancing in the fireplace. She imagined she could see shapes and faces in them. Her body glistened with droplets of water. She drew the towel across her back, then down along her front and dried herself off. The terrible chill was beginning to leave her body as her skin warmed and she began to feel more relaxed. Reaching out with her hands she gripped the mug. It smelled so good. She slowly put the mug to her lips.

Hesitating, she wondered was it a trap, could it be filled with poison? After all, were they not the enemy of the seas and the wild folk? Yet this nusham seemed to be kind, he had a warm voice and kind eyes. He had given her shelter from the storm. She decided to risk it. She began to sip the warm chocolate. It tasted sweet and when she swallowed she felt a warming sensation. Gulping it down she quickly emptied the mug. Then she eyed the biscuits. They felt hard to the touch. Bringing one to her mouth she bit on it. It too, tasted sweet, but in a different way from the chocolate. She could feel it melting in her mouth. She chewed and chewed, then swallowed it. Then she finished the rest of biscuits on the plate.

Looking around the room, she saw her comb on the shelf. She picked it up then kissed it. She felt it must be a good omen. She placed it back on the shelf. She began to feel sleepy. The sofa was not like her bed in the palace but it felt good as she sat down on the cushions. She lay her head back on another cushion and used it as a pillow. She looked at the fire and the flickering shadows. Soon sleep began to creep over her and before long she lay sound asleep.

* * *

Jimmy Talbot lay in his darkened bed listening to the rain pattering on his bedroom window, wondering who was that poor young girl in the next room. If he didn't know better he would have called her a changeling, a fairy child.

Chapter 12

Jimmy awoke with the warm sunlight streaming in the window on to his face. He blinked and shielded his eyes from the brilliant blaze of sunshine. Easing himself out of his bed, he scratched his beard, then threw on some clothes. Suddenly he remembered the events of the night before and his surprise midnight caller. He hurried out to the sitting room. Had he dreamt the whole thing? There was nobody to be seen. The sofa cushions still held the shape of someone who had slept there. He picked up the mug. It was empty; only traces of the chocolate on the rim. The few biscuits he had left were eaten.

'Hello!' He called lightly in case she might be in the bathroom or upstairs. There was no answer. He was a bit disappointed. He would have loved to talk to her however briefly, to find out if she was in any trouble. Had she run away from home? It was totally unnatural that a young girl should call to a stranger in the middle of the night without a stitch of clothes on her.

He opened the kitchen door. There was a faint sound of the sea. Thankfully the storm had blown itself out and no tiles had fallen from the roof, which usually happened during a storm. He looked out; the sun was illuminating the flat calm sea. He could hear the croaking call of a raven, as he caught sight of it flying along the cliffs. The raven was probably hoping to pick up some casualties of last night's storm, there would be a lot of dead birds because of the ferocity of the storm.

Then he saw the young girl sitting among clumps of sea thrift near the lighthouse. He gave a sigh of relief and called to her:

'Good morning, young lady.' Afraid she might run away, the old man approached gingerly. He likened her to one of the small migrant birds that might seek the shelter of the lighthouse in stormy weather.

Emerald turned and smiled back. She looked at the burly nusham approaching, but didn't feel frightened. He moved beside her and sat on a nearby rock. She looked at his face. He had a sculptured but serene face and was soft spoken as he asked her did she sleep well. Emerald nodded, looking at his thick white beard and thick eyebrows. She wanted to touch them.

He introduced himself: 'I'm Jimmy Talbot'. He thrust out his hand.

Emerald offered hers. His big hand clasped hers and shook it warmly.

'Thank you for giving me shelter last night,' she said.

'Oh, think nothing of it,' he smiled broadly. 'But you did give me a bit of a start calling so late.'

'I'm so sorry, it was selfish of me,' she replied.

'Not at all, dear child. It's just that when you have lived alone for as long as I have, with only the wind, rocks and sea for company and the occasional wild bird, you develop a fertile imagination.' He laughed. 'I was convinced you might have been some lost soul, a drowned sailor disturbed by the storm and roused from your resting-place at the bottom of the sea.'

Emerald smiled. She looked out seawards at the water caressing the coves.

'The sea is not angry today,' she said softly. 'Perhaps it didn't want me to leave.'

Jimmy reflected on her words. It was a telling remark, but what was she saying? That she had come from the sea? That was too fantastical an idea to believe in the early morning sunshine.

'You still haven't told me your name,' he probed.

'I am Emerald,' she replied.

'Emerald! A beautiful name. It suits you.' He looked deep into her eyes. 'Your eyes are like the sea, full of mystery.'

She stared warmly back. He sensed dialogue in the silent gaze but could not fathom it. The sound of the seabirds could be heard calling from the cliffs.

'Listen, young lady. I don't know about you, but if I don't get a good breakfast in me, I can't function properly. I need my morning fuel, and my caffeine injection as my nephew calls it. Hopefully he's coming to visit at the weekend; you can meet him if you stay around.' He stood up. 'Oh, I'm stiff'. He rubbed his knees. 'Come on, young Emerald. We can talk some more over breakfast.'

She followed him down the slopes.

'It's an amazing sensation walking on the soft grass with these legs.'

Jimmy stopped in his tracks and looked at her, not knowing what to say.

'Legs are amazing. I'm getting used to them,' she continued, bending over to look at them. 'Your legs are different, more bow-legged.'

'Thanks very much,' he retorted in mock annoyance. 'Having carried as much as I have over the years it's a wonder I don't have little stumps. See that wall over there beside the lighthouse? I helped to build that with these.' He raised up his hands proudly. 'It's still standing, despite the wind, the rain and the occasional giant wave beating against it. A good cut-stone granite wall.'

'You are clever,' she remarked.

'Well, thank you.' He smiled, feeling pleased with himself.

'Only, less remarks about my bandy legs, please' he chuckled.

They went inside the house.

'First things first. Fill the kettle.' Then he got a bathrobe for her to wear. 'Put this on.'

She watched him go about the business of making the breakfast. He opened a can and poured orange juice from it.

'Well, I don't mind saying, Emerald, it's great to have your company for breakfast.' She smiled up at him. 'You have to pull your weight around here,' he said, handing her a bag of muesli and some bowls. 'Here, put them on the table.' Then pulling open a drawer he took out some cutlery and handed it to her. 'Milk's in the fridge.' She looked blank. 'Fridge. You know what a fridge looks like!' he remarked. She gave a puzzled look. 'Okay my dear, it's your first morning here, so I don't expect you to know your way about this place. You just go on inside and I'll join you shortly.'

He busied himself making scrambled eggs and toast. Emerald began to have a good look around the sitting room in the morning light. There were pictures hanging on the walls, records, ornaments, carvings, bookcases full of books, chairs and a wooden floor with rugs on it. A barn owl stared a glassy-eyed stare from a dome. All the pictures showed ships. She looked from picture to picture: a frigate, a man-of-war, a cutter, a sixteen-gun sloop-of-war brig, *Shannon* a clipper ship, the *Mirage* a 965 tonne clipper, *Cornwallis* an iron clipper and a picture of the great tea race of 1872 between the *Cutty Sark* and the *Thermopylae*.

'Right,' he said brightly. 'We're all set. First let's have some cereal.' They sat down opposite each other. Emerald watched him shake the muesli into his bowl, then pour milk over it from the jug. He indicated to her to do the same. She smiled back and repeated exactly what he did. Then taking a dessert spoon he scooped it up and put it into his mouth. 'Mmm,' he sighed in a satisfied manner.

Emerald did the same with the spoon, only took a bigger spoonful. Ramming it into her mouth, her cheeks bulged with the big mouthful of cereal. She tried to make the sound he did but some cereal clusters shot out of her mouth.

He laughed loudly.

'Perhaps you should take smaller mouthfuls.'

He mimed with his spoon, taking up a smaller portion. Emerald nodded in agreement, then picked the particles from the table that had escaped from her mouth. After the cereal was eaten he brought in the scrambled eggs on toast. Placing one plate in front of her, he then sat down with his. Taking up the knife and fork, he instructed her to repeat the same thing. As she watched him work the knife and fork, then put the food into his mouth, she laughed aloud. He looked puzzled.

'You eat like a lizard,' she said. 'The way your tongue comes out for the food.'

'Thanks very much. First I have bow legs, now I eat like a lizard.'

'Oh, I didn't mean to be critical. I was only observing.'

'That's all right,' he chuckled. 'I was only checking that the food wasn't too hot,' he excused his behaviour. 'I suppose living on your own one gets into odd habits,' he mused.

Emerald ate the scrambled egg and toast.

'Verdict?' He insisted.

'Oh lovely, very tasty. I've never had it before,' she added. 'I normally just nibble algae, but since I've become a kind of nusham my appetite has improved.'

'Listen, young lady, I don't know what planet you dropped

in from or whether my nephew put you up to playing this prank on me, but you are very good. I am totally confused.'

Emerald watched him pour tea for the two of them. He sighed: 'So you enjoyed the free-range eggs? I get them from a grand lady who lives a few miles from here.'

'I've eaten eggs?' said Emerald in shocked tones. 'But what about the parents? Wouldn't they mind?'

'Parents?' He scratched his head. 'Oh, you mean the hens? No, that's what they do, the hens lay the eggs. They're not wild birds . . . I didn't take them from the cliffs, if that's what you are implying.' Then he stopped himself. 'What the Dickens! Here I am justifying myself for eating scrambled eggs.' He let out a deep sigh. 'Listen, young lady. You'll have to come clean with me. Why are you here, and why do you act as if you're from another planet?'

'You have that look – as if you are cross with me – just like my mother and father get when they are cross.'

He reached out his arms and clasped her hands in his.

'Listen Emerald, dear. I'm not cross, only confused. I'm sitting here having breakfast with a beautiful young lady who acts as if she's never seen the inside of a house before.' He stood up and went into his bedroom. Emerald began to feel anxious. She looked over at the fish tank that had some creatures from a rock pool.

'Here, young lady.' He said, handing her a shirt. 'I don't want someone seeing you walking around naked here. You'll get arrested. We both will.' He looked to the heavens. 'And there's a pair of shorts, my nephew left here some time back. He won't be needing them.'

Emerald slipped out of the bathrobe.

'That's right, put the shirt over your head,' he instructed.

The young woman put the clothes on.

'I haven't worn that shirt for some time. It won't fit me, I've got too fat!' He grabbed hold of his stomach.

'They feel nice, thank you,' said Emerald. 'Everything is so new to me, it's amazing.'

'Now, before I went into my room . . .'

'Oh, could I just say . . . ?' Emerald interrupted.

'Yes, what is it?' he wondered.

'Well,' she said. 'Your fish tank is lovely.'

'Oh, thank you,' he replied, a little puzzled. 'Simple to make . . . some perspex or plate glass and sealer and some creatures from the seashore. I love to watch them,' he smiled. 'As interesting as any exotic aquarium you would buy in a pet shop, and a lot cheaper,' he added.

'Only . . . the blenny could do with a mate and the shore crab feels it's time she was returned to sea, as she is getting a lot bigger.'

Jimmy stared at her, wide-eyed.

'What about the others?' he retorted in disbelief.

'Oh, they seem happy enough; they say you look after them very well, only the anemones would like to see more shrimps. Of course we know why that is,' said Emerald smiling. 'They just want to catch them.'

'I think I need a fresh pot of tea,' said the old man. 'This is all too much. *You* can talk to little sea creatures?'

'Oh yes,' said Emerald. 'I can communicate with all creatures, large and small.'

'I'm going mad,' Jimmy mumbled. 'It must be from living too long on my own.'

He went into the kitchen and made some more tea. Emerald went out after him. She put her arms around him and hugged him from behind. He could feel her head pressed against his back and her hands held tightly around his chest.

'I was right about you,' she said warmly. 'Yesterday I thought I was swimming into the jaws of death. Since I've arrived on the land you have shown me nothing but kindness. I was right to choose you. Dorad was doubtful, but he went along with my wishes. He loves me.'

The old man turned and looked at this mysterious young girl. 'You chose me? What does that mean?' He broke away gently from her embrace. 'I don't want this hot tea burning you.'

They returned to the dining table. He poured tea for the two of them and put milk into the two mugs. She watched, her eyes always curious. He swigged some tea then stared at her.

'Who or what are you, my child? I need to know.' His voice was quiet but determined.

'Have you something I could draw with?' she asked.

He stretched over and took a pencil and a notepad from the bookshelf and he passed them over to her. She took the pencil and began to draw something. He watched with great interest as he drank down his tea. When finished she turned the notepad towards him. He slowly picked up the notepad and there on the page was a lovely sketch of a mermaid. He looked up at Emerald. She smiled back nervously.

'A mermaid!' he gasped, in utter amazement.

'Yes,' she responded. 'I was told to tell nobody, at least no nusham and here I am telling you, the first nusham I meet. Because I trust you. I don't think there is any badness in you. I only see goodness.'

His eyes filled up and a tear ran freely down his face.

'A mermaid!' he smiled.

'Please don't be sad about the idea,' Emerald pleaded.

'Oh, I'm not sad, dear child. I'm happy, confused. I've loved the sea all my life, I still do. It's full of secrets and now here you are, a mermaid. The stuff of myths and legends.'

'Oh, the sea is still a mystery to me as well. It's my home, or was,' she added. 'It's like my secret mother, my friend, my lover, my guardian. Yet sometimes it scares me, especially when it's angry.'

Jimmy poured more tea out for himself and wiped his eyes with his handkerchief. 'A MERMAID! A MERMAID!' he repeated quietly. 'How did you choose me?' he asked warmly.

'We used to watch you work along the shoreline, looking for things, driftwood mainly.'

'Who's we?' he enquired.

'Dorad, my dolphin. He is such a dear friend . . . he's always there for me. He's got me out of many a troublesome situation. He brings me gifts too, from the bottom of the sea. It was he who left the comb on the shoreline. I hoped and prayed you would find it.'

The old man rushed over and picked up the jewelled comb.

'This is yours?'

Emerald nodded.

'Here it is back, all cleaned up.' He offered it to her.

'No, I would like you to keep it,' she retorted.

'I couldn't keep a mermaid's comb.'

Emerald took the comb and pushed it in her hair.

'That's much better than lying on a shelf,' he smiled.

'Well since you returned it to me I shall bring you something I found in the sea. It will be my gift to you.'

'Your gift to me is yourself. You are welcome to stay here and call it your home for as long as you choose to stay.'

Chapter 13

'Let's go for a walk. I need to clear my head. We can take the cliff walk. There are spectacular views from there. Oh! You don't have shoes for your feet.'

Emerald smiled. 'I'm fine.' She held his hands. 'Everything is fine. You are coming to terms with me and I'm coming to terms with a nusham.'

'Yes I suppose so.' He headed for the kitchen exit then stopped. 'Hold on a minute. What's a nusham? It sounds like a nuisance.'

'You are nusham to us,' replied Emerald.

'Listen young lady, we are humans! Human beings! I am a man and you are a girl, well, a young woman. So you better get used to calling us humans or people or men or whatever, but not nusham. Do you get the message?'

'I do,' said Emerald trying to stifle a laugh.

'And, of course,' he added, 'I cannot introduce you as a mermaid. You will be a student friend who has come here to study marine life. I know it's a bit of a white lie, since you probably know more than any of us, but it will save any awkward questions in the future. Oh, my head is spinning! Let's go,' he bellowed.

Out they went and headed for the path that led up to the cliffs.

The noise of the gulls was almost deafening as they began their ascent. The old man walked silently ahead following along the narrow winding dirt-track. He stopped to gaze seawards and admire the raw beauty of the sea.

'I never tire of looking at her. I should have been a sailor or a fisherman, making a living from the sea,' he grinned. 'Oh, I've sailed the seas and worked my passage on cargo ships that were heading for some exotic places. That was a lifetime ago, when I was young with not a care in the world.' He turned to her and continued: 'Most of us nusham, I mean humans . . .' Emerald laughed. '. . . have only a blurred idea of what life is like out there in the salty depths.' She nodded in agreement.

They moved further along the steep cliffs. A light cool breeze from the sea made Emerald's hair blow around her face.

'Look,' he said, pointing to rocks that rose in jagged splendour. 'That's called Eagle Rock. It looks just like an eagle is about to be born out of the rock. Can you see the shape of the head and the beak?' he said excitedly. Emerald nodded. 'I'm always seeing faces and images in rocks and in the clouds. I get that from my father, Lord rest his soul,' he added. 'He was always pointing out pink castles in the sky or chariots being pulled by white horses. My mother was the sensible one in our family. Had her feet firmly planted on the ground while my father's head was in the clouds. Listen, I'm talking too much. You don't want to be listening to the ramblings of an old man.'

'No, I love to hear you talk. You remind me of Grypus or Murgen.'

'And who, pray tell, are they?' he wondered.

'One is a dear friend, well I only got to know him recently, but we are very close. He is a bull seal.'

'Oh, a bull seal! You sure know how to pay one a compliment. And the other is a shark, no doubt?'

She laughed loudly. 'No. Murgen was my grandmother; she was very wise. We called her Grandmother Nature.'

'Well at least she was wise,' he smirked. 'Was?' he quizzed.

'Yes. She died recently, sadly,' said Emerald.

'Oh, I'm sorry to hear that. I suppose she was a mermaid too?' He refrained from mocking.

'Oh yes, one of the oldest in the Emerald Kingdom, as old as the empress,' she added.

'We have a lot to talk about later, young lady, but first we must walk. I try to get in a good walk at least once a day.'

Jimmy pointed out another rock stack along a narrow sheltered section of the cliff. They could see the sea surge into the tiny cracks and crevices of the fractured rocks. There were several overhanging rocks ready to collapse into the water.

'Winter time here can be very tricky, with the strong winds and unremitting assaults by the sea. A lot of the cliff face gets eroded. From my house I have heard rocks crashing into the sea. It can be quite scary at times. I wonder how much bombardment this section can take before the whole section breaks away. Then it will be impossible to get over to see where the birds are breeding. Oh!' he added. 'It might not be in my lifetime.'

From their vantage point they could see the beach very clearly. Jimmy put his arm around Emerald and with the other hand he pointed to the strandline, the ribbon of weed and litter left after the sea had turned.

'Down among that marine debris is a treasure trove for me. There, of course, is where I found your comb.'

Emerald pulled it out of her hair and mimed to it, as if there might have been different ones.

'That's the one,' he grinned.

The young woman pulled her hair and twirled and shaped it on top of her head and put the comb back to keep it in position. Jimmy rummaged in his pockets and took out something, clenched in his fist. He asked her to guess what was in his hand. Emerald said she had no idea. He opened his large hand and in the palm were two brown shiny objects.

'I bet you haven't seen them before. There again, maybe you have,' he said a bit disappointed. Emerald picked up the shiny objects. They felt hard to the touch. 'Give up?' he smiled. 'They are macuna and entada, sea beans all the way from the Caribbean and Central America. I found them down there, strewn along the seashore. I've found quite a number over the years.' he said, all pleased with himself.

Then he produced two mint sweets from his other pocket. He unwrapped the paper from one and popped it into his mouth. Emerald was given the other. 'I bet you haven't tasted a sweet before?' She shook her head. 'Good, hey?'

'Good,' she replied as she moved the minty sweet about in her mouth. On the faraway beach Emerald could see some kelp fronds, floating near the shore. They brought back warm memories of the visit to the kelp forest with Dorad, Lutra and Grypus.

*   *   *

Gulls hung in the clear cloudless sky: great black-backed, lesser black-backed and herring gulls. Some stood not too far away, but as the old man and young woman approached they took to the wing and joined the other circling gulls. The raucous calls echoed around the cliffs. In the calm seas below, guillemots weaved over the surface. Some would suddenly dive underwater, trying to catch a fish.

'The guillemots don't build a nest,' said the old man to Emerald. 'They lay a pear-shaped egg so it won't roll off the cliffs.'

Emerald told him about seeing the young fledgelings leap from the cliffs into the sea under the cover of darkness.

'I've never seen that,' he remarked. 'But I rescued one from a discarded piece of fishing net. It gave me a peck for my trouble,' he grinned.

They walked further along the cliffs through carpets of sea thrift. 'This place is a haven for seabirds. Ah, look,' he said with delight, pointing at an abandoned nest. 'It's a raven's nest, I'm sure of it.' He got down on all fours to get a closer look. Emerald did the same. The nest was below an overhanging rock. It was cupped with sticks, cemented with mud and moss and the inside was lined with sheep's wool and hair. 'They breed early,' he said. 'The young must be fledged by now.'

He told her how in the early part of the year, in mid-March, he happened upon the nest. Having been disturbed by accident the female flew off, croaking loudly. Then he spotted the nest from where she had flown. A clutch of four lovely greenish-blue eggs was visible. The female was soon joined by the male and they circled overhead, showing their annoyance. 'I quickly moved on. I didn't want the eggs to get cold. All the young were successfully hatched out, I'm glad to say.'

In the distance, to the left of where they crouched, lay an undulating landscape of farms ribboned by hedgerows. It all looked so beautiful to Emerald, who was seeing it all for the first time. Thickets of gorse grew up along the side of the hills. The beautiful coconut fragrance from its yellow flowers hung in the air.

Emerald stretched out her arms and took in deep breaths. 'Oh, I did not imagine the land could be so beautiful.'

'Lots more to see, my child.'

In the glare of the midday sun they sat on a great rock that bulged out from the spongey turf. There they watched the antics of puffins with their comical multi-coloured beaks as they whirred around, moving in and out to sea. Some adults stood at the entrance to their burrows encouraging the young to come out. Jimmy told her how on several occasions he had seen the puffins chase away a resident rabbit, then take over his burrow. They would extend the burrow by digging with their powerful beaks and then shuffling the soil out with their feet. Usually one egg was laid and about six weeks later a chick would emerge. Jimmy and Emerald could hear the whirring wings of the puffins as they flew in tight formation.

On the steepest part of the cliffs kittiwakes sat with their young. Some were still brooding in their cup nests made of seaweed, grass and moss. At the beginning of the breeding season they fashioned their nests with their feet. This cup shape then hardened against the cliff face. Three eggs were laid and when the young hatched out they developed claws to cling safely to the ledges. They constantly called out *Kittiwake! Kittiwake!*

Jimmy watched Emerald as she looked at everything in wide-eyed admiration.

'I wish I could look again at the world with your eyes,' he said smiling. 'If only we all could,' he added, with some irony.

'I need to swim,' she said brightly. 'Will you join me?'

'Oh, I can't swim,' he declared. 'Never got around to it, learning I mean.'

'I'll teach you,' she said. Her eyes twinkled.

'Oh, I'm too old,' he insisted.

'Oh, please you would love it,' she pleaded.

'Well, we'll see,' he said doubtfully. 'First let's go back and have a spot of lunch. This fresh air gives me a powerful appetite.'

*   *   *

They returned to Sandpiper House. Emerald pointed at the sign on the wall of the house,

'It's getting a bit faded now. I must touch it up. Again, a gift from the sea. I was going to call the house Driftwood, then I spotted some purple sandpipers one winter morning among the seaweed. So hence the name. Do you like the painting?'

Emerald nodded.

'Painting is something I dabble at when I'm not carving. When you are retired you have a lot of time on your hands. I am one of those people who must be doing something. It was my nephew who started me painting. He bought me some watercolour paints and brushes, as well as a book on the subject. And gave me a few tips on how to do washes and mix colours. It was one of the best presents I ever got, apart from the binoculars and telescope my colleagues bought me on my retirement.'

Inside the house Jimmy made some cheese and tomato sandwiches and opened a tin of tomato soup. Pouring it into a saucepan, he let it heat slowly. Emerald filled the electric kettle and flicked on the switch.

'You're learning fast,' he grinned.

After their lunch he showed Emerald some of his sketches and watercolours. She was very impressed.

'You must teach me to paint like that, please, and in return I will teach you to swim,' she offered.

'That's a promise.' He extended his hand, and they shook and laughed.

He showed her some things he had bought or found. 'This is a fossil of an ammonite.' Then moving around the room he continued. 'Do you know what this is?' He asked, showing her a stuffed wader on a perch. It didn't have a glass case like the owl.

'It's a curlew,' she smiled, touching its long bill. 'I prefer it alive,' she retorted.

'Well, true,' he agreed. 'But it's nice to sketch.'

Emerald picked up an ear-shaped shell.

'That's an ormer shell. It's related to the limpet.'

She examined the lovely mother-of-pearl.

'Ormer comes from the French, I read somewhere. It means "ear of the sea": *oreille de mer*, sounds good,' he laughed.

There were other shells in a glass case: keyhole limpet shells, tusk shells, venus shells, painted topshells, cowries, razor shells, dog whelks, periwinkles and scallop shells. Emerald also examined various pots, ornamental plates and a brass bell. She lifted up the heavy brass bell. It sounded.

'The bell I got as a swap for a seal carving I did. It's from a ship! A good swap, don't you think?' Emerald nodded.

Then she picked up a faded photograph of a slim, handsome man with black hair and a beard. There was something familiar about him. Then she exclaimed loudly: 'It's you!'

'It's me all right, a century ago.'

'Are you a century?' she enquired.

'No, I'm just kidding. But I feel like it sometimes. Time is the only thing that beats us all in the end.' He sighed. 'Listen, if I sit here I'll begin to doze off, so if you want to have that swim, we'd better go.'

He grabbed two bath towels and an old pair of black boxer shorts. They headed on a different track down to the seashore. Emerald could hardly contain her excitement as she neared the water. Throwing off her clothes, she ran towards the sea.

Jimmy looked around to see if there was anyone about. He'd have to get her a swimsuit before the day was out. The wind had picked up. It was now blowing in from the sea.

Emerald danced into the water, then dived below a wave. Jimmy fumbled with a towel to remove his clothes and put on his shorts. He felt a bit silly. He scratched his white hairy chest and sucked in his stomach, then released it. Emerald was so far out in the water he could barely see her.

This was the first time in years he had walked barefoot along the sand. He slowly made his way to the water, hoping he wouldn't catch a chill. The sun was still warm but white clouds were moving in from the sea. Emerald was frolicking in the water, bobbing up and down, then disappearing for several minutes before appearing on the surface again. He was reminded of young seals he had watched from the lighthouse doing the same. Then she moved gracefully just below the surface, her head barely visible.

Sandwich terns flew overhead as Jimmy stood at the water's edge. He scooped up some water; it felt cold. He splashed his face with the salty water, then crossed himself.

'It's wonderful!' Emerald shouted, beckoning him to come in.

Gingerly he entered, walking in up to his waist. The cold water reaching his shorts made him shiver. Emerald was beside him in an instant. She helped him ease himself into the water. He felt a mixture of fear and excitement.

'Just relax,' she said in a soothing voice . . . He lay spread-eagled on his back, amazed he hadn't sunk to the bottom.

'Look at the beautiful blue sky with the white fluffy clouds drifting slowly by.'

Feeling the security of her hands in the middle of his back, he began to relax. He could feel his whole body succumb to a state of complete relaxation. It was as if he had become part of the calm blue water. He floated in the hushed silence of the sea in complete tranquillity.

With watchful eyes Emerald let the old man float by himself, moving slowly in the wave-lapped water. After a few minutes Emerald helped him to turn on to his front. He took a breath and lay face down on the water. This he did for a few seconds before gasping for air. After a time she brought him out of the water.

'I think that's enough for one day.' she said.

'Oh that felt good! Really!' he beamed.

'I'm glad,' she smiled, returning to the water's edge.

Stretching out his towel on the sand Jimmy sat down, then lay out on it. Vivid memories came to him of his childhood, his family and friends, where they played on the beach, built sand castles and had picnics on long summer days. Tears ran from his eyes.

Emerald was back in the sea. She leaped over some waves, dived under others, and let the force of the waves drive her to the shore, tossing and twisting in the white foam. She was in her element. She stood up, dived back into the water and torpedoed out to sea, twisting and turning in her subdued blue world. She surfaced and lay out on the water, allowing the waves to envelop her. Emerald never imagined that the transition would be so easy; she had adapted so well to the land life and she still had the sea close by.

Eventually the sea brought her back towards the shoreline and tossed her on the wet sand. Lying there on her back in the warm sunlight, with the surf washing over her ankles, she drifted into a beautiful sleep.

*   *   *

Emerald awoke and lolled about and stretched luxuriously on the soft sand. The sea had retreated several metres. She sat up and looked over at the old man; he was sleeping soundly. She got dressed and strolled up along the beach, enjoying the way her feet made an impression in the sand. She looked back at her footprint trail. Further up the beach she could see a redshank searching the rotting seaweed on the shoreline for sand hoppers and ragworms. Nearer to the water's edge a curlew probed for lugworms with its long curved bill. Emerald could get the strong smell of the seaweed as she passed along. Hopping hordes of sand hoppers leaped ahead of her footsteps.

The storm had brought in a sizeable amount of driftwood, weather-worn branches and roots, a plank with goose barnacles attached to it, plastic crates, several bottles of plastic and glass, a wooden box and some fishing net. Flocks of starlings and some turnstones were disturbed and flew over her head only to return to the bleached seaweed lower down the beach. Out to sea a cormorant was drying its wings in the breeze.

Near the far end of the beach on the wave-washed rocks, an oystercatcher searched for food. With its bright orange bill it hammered a mussel, chiselled the fleshy meat free, then gulped it down. A prying herring gull flew over hoping to snatch an easy meal, but the oystercatcher was too quick for it. The gull flew away in annoyance to a different stretch of rock.

Emerald decided she had better return to the old man. She stroked his nose lightly with a feather she had found. His nose twitched and he blinked awake and gave a loud yawn. Emerald was bent over him smiling.

'What time is it?' he asked, then looked for his watch. He had slept for over two hours. He quickly got to his feet. 'That was the best sleep I had in ages, and the first time I've slept outdoors in a very long time. Turn around, young lady. I want a bit of privacy.'

When he was dressed they walked slowly along the beach back to the house. She linked her arm in his and asked had he any more of those sweet things in his pocket? He produced two more mints. As soon as they arrived at the house he got his car from the garage. Emerald was a bit nervous when the engine started up.

'No need to alarm yourself. We need to go into the village to get some groceries and some suitable clothes for you, including a swimsuit.'

Emerald got into the car and sat close to him. They headed down the road to the village which was about eight miles away. Along the narrow road Emerald began to feel nervous again and snuggled up to the old man.

'Just sit back and watch the world go by,' he reassured her.

He told her of the different animals they saw in the fields as they passed by: the cows, the sheep, a horse and a donkey. He named some of the trees: the beech, the rowan, the horse-chestnut, and the oak. Two children passed them on bicycles. Jimmy waved out the window at them.

'They look lovely, those small nusham . . . I mean humans,' she corrected herself.

'You mean children,' he laughed.

'What were they holding in their hands?' she enquired.

'Ice creams,' he answered. 'And if you've never tasted one before, which I'm sure you haven't, then you're in for a real treat.'

Arriving in the village Emerald could not believe her eyes. So many houses stuck together and so many people moving about. They were all different shapes. Some were big, others small; some very fat, others very thin; some had beards, while others were bald.

Jimmy parked the car and they walked down the street. Emerald clung tightly to him. He patted her arm, amused at her reaction. Then they entered a small supermarket. He took up some bread, beans, cheese, rashers and sausages, apples, bananas, oranges, milk, tea and a cake and put them in the basket.

Emerald looked around at other girls her own age. They were very pretty. They passed by talking to each other. The check-out girl greeted Jimmy warmly and they talked about the weather. He introduced Emerald to Sharon. They smiled at each other and shook hands. They returned to the car to put the groceries inside, then Jimmy led the way to a clothes shop. Again, the woman knew him and greeted him warmly. He whispered something in her ear. She nodded then asked Emerald to follow her. She was reluctant but the old man insisted, promising he'd stay right where he was. After a time Emerald returned to him wearing a T-shirt with a dolphin on it, a pair of jeans, and sparkling white runners on her feet.

'That's better.' He smiled and paid for the other items of clothing that the assistant recommended, including a colourful swimsuit. Then in the chemist shop he purchased a toothbrush, toothpaste, a hairbrush, shampoo and a beach towel.

'That should do for the moment. Let's pop into the Cobweb Tearooms.'

They sat down at a window table and Jimmy ordered two cappuccinos and two strawberry gateaux. Emerald looked around at the different people enjoying their cakes and tea. She tasted the coffee. It was nice but not as nice as the hot chocolate. Then she tucked into the cake. It was deliciously sweet.

An old gentleman came over to Jimmy and patted him on the back.

'That's bad for you,' he quipped, looking at him eating the cake.

'Sure how come all the nice things are bad for you?' Jimmy retorted.

He then introduced Benny Browne to Emerald. She stood up and hugged him. He was taken aback by her warm embrace.

'Well it's not every day a pretty young girl gives me a hug,' he smiled.

Jimmy explained awkwardly that she was the only daughter of a distant relation who had come visiting: 'A student of the sea, marine world, you know what I mean.'

'Yes,' said Benny. 'That sounds interesting. Listen, why don't you two come over to the Sailor's Wharf tonight, we're playing there.'

'Well . . . my niece here is underage,' he offered as an excuse.

'That won't be a problem if she doesn't start on the whiskey,' said Benny winking at her. 'Come for nine o'clock and I'll buy her an orange juice. And one for you too,' he laughed. 'Well, I'd better be on my way I have to collect my granddaughter from her dancing lesson. See you tonight.'

'He seems nice,' said Emerald.

'Oh he is,' said Jimmy. 'I've known Benny for years. He used to work in the Met Office, he was a weatherman. He's retired like me. A good musician and singer, he plays the fiddle. Yes, you might enjoy listening to some traditional music.'

'Oh I love music,' said Emerald. 'So do all my clan.'

'Well, this is a good area for musicians,' said Jimmy. 'You could throw a stick anywhere around here and you would hit six musicians,' he chuckled.

After they had finished they headed for home but not before Jimmy insisted Emerald had an ice cream. They ate them in the car on the way home. Emerald really enjoyed her ice cream but felt very full after it.

* * *

That evening they drove to the Sailor's Wharf. It was a thatch-roofed pub in the Tudor style of design. Emerald sat at a dark oak table with Jimmy. He was nursing a pint of Guinness while Emerald had a glass of orange juice. There was a large gathering of people there.

'Mostly tourists,' whispered Jimmy in her ear.

Then the musicians arrived and settled themselves in a corner.

'They're called the Village Fiddlers, all local,' he informed her.

The men began to tune their instruments, the fiddles and the banjos. They also had a concertina and a bodhran. They began to play and people clapped and joined in the singing. Emerald enjoyed the music; it was different from anything she had heard before. Benny Browne winked at her.

It was hard to believe all the terrible things she had heard about the nusham, now that she was living among them. They all seemed so friendly and kind. Perhaps there were different kinds of nusham, ones she had never met who were the dangerous ones. Then Benny Browne called on his good friend Jimmy 'Sparrow' Talbot to sing a song.

'I knew this was coming,' he sighed.

'You can sing?' she asked.

'Not well,' he replied. 'But if I don't he'll hound me all night.'

Jimmy stood up. People applauded, especially the locals who shouted words of encouragement. He took a sip from his drink, which brought loud cheers and laughter. Then he cleared his throat. He was glad there were no microphones or other sound systems; the area was too intimate for that. He began to sing a sea shanty about a whaling expedition. When he finished there were loud cheers and calls for more. But he sat down; one song was enough. He looked at Emerald, then began to feel a little awkward for his song has been about catching and killing the great whales. He suddenly realised how inappropriate it was.

Emerald just smiled, said how much she enjoyed it, and then said she would like to sing. Jimmy looked surprised at her unexpected request but if she wanted to sing by heavens she was going to. He stood up and asked for a bit of hush, as his niece wanted to sing. There was even louder applause that someone had agreed to sing without all the coaxing that was usually necessary. Emerald slowly got to her feet. The background chat was stilled as the villagers eyed the beautiful young stranger.

'I would like to sing this for my grandmother and for all my absent friends who are at sea.'

Jimmy hoped she wouldn't say anything more that might reveal her true identity. She closed her eyes and began with a long clear sound. Then as she sang, a great calm enveloped the listeners. The beautiful voice that emanated from her mouth was thrilling. Her high silvery tones moved like the wind through the reeds. The musical sounds seemed to show the dark clouds parting to reveal a golden harvest moon. It was as if you could hear a waterfall enter a slow-moving river. It was like the slow wingbeats of a great bird. It was like a rainbow of sounds. The whole room was charged with such an exquisite serenity that some cried freely. Her voice had proclaimed all the light, beauty and harmony that may enter the purest of hearts. It became a doorway of light, inviting them to enter into the great mystery.

When she had finished there was a long silence. People just stared in wonderment at the beautiful young girl with the glorious voice. Jimmy was stunned. Then he recovered himself, and grabbing Emerald by the arm he quickly ushered her out of the pub. When people realised what was happening they cheered and applauded loudly, calling for more.

He got to his car and let her in without wasting any time. Within minutes they were heading out of the car park for home. He said not a word to her as they travelled along the dark windy roads. Finally he could see the lighthouse with its warm light piercing the darkness, always a welcome beacon for Jimmy Talbot. He had many fond memories of his days as a keeper. When the car came to a halt in the driveway, Emerald touched his shoulder.

'I've done something wrong? I've hurt you, I've embarrassed you in front of your friends? What is it? What's wrong?' she pleaded.

He bent over the steering wheel with his hands on his face and sobbed uncontrollably.

Emerald began to cry too. 'What? What?' she pleaded. 'Tell me what I did to upset you so much.'

He turned to her, wiping his eyes with his sleeves. He whispered. 'You haven't hurt me, my child. You are like a gift, like a prayer.' He sobbed again. 'I don't know what I'm trying to say. You have made me whole, all in one single day. I feel so privileged to be in your company. It's as if you are an angel of the sea,' he smiled, 'if that's possible. You radiate such goodness.'

She smiled. 'I thought I had done something terrible. I thought you hated my voice.'

They laughed, cried and laughed again.

When they got inside the house the phone rang. It was Chris, his nephew, saying that he was sorry he could not make it over because he was going on tour to Europe with the band, but that he would make contact on his return visit. Jimmy was a little disappointed; he so wanted Chris to meet young Emerald.

Chapter 14

Over the next few months Jimmy Talbot and his beautiful visitor from the sea got to know each other really well. Their relationship became very close and special, like a grandfather with his granddaughter or an uncle with his niece. Emerald experienced a warmth and security that gave her the confidence to explore further the world of the land people.

Emerald was accepted into the life of the village community. Of course no one ever got to know her real identity. She became very popular especially with the young people. She would visit the local schools and tell them about the sea and the seashore; her fascinating talks worked in very well with the environmental classes.

The local library was quick to recognise her talents too and asked her to become involved in storytime sessions with younger children after school. Emerald told wonderful stories about the sea and about strange creatures that lived there. The young children especially loved when she told them about the mermaid kingdom and the magical palace hidden in the depths of the sea.

Emerald was also offered part-time work as a swimming instructor. Young and old joined her classes and learned how to swim. She was so patient and understanding with them that they learned to relax and not be fearful of the water. Some even came just to watch her swim the lengths of the pool when the classes were finished. There were comments that she could easily enter for the Olympics, she was such a strong natural swimmer, with grace and agility.

But what she enjoyed doing most was singing. A big crowd

would be guaranteed at the Sailor's Wharf if it was rumoured Emerald was singing that evening.

Having earned some money, she could bring Jimmy out for the occasional meal in a restaurant. Often she would buy him something new, like a new shirt or a book he liked, especially books about lighthouse keepers or seafarers and things pertaining to the sea. He would always scold her for wasting her money on him, but she knew he appreciated it. Most of their evenings were spent sitting around the fire, listening to music and reading. Emerald would always sing at least one song each evening; it was almost compulsory. Since Emerald loved singing it suited them both. In return she would ask him to read something from his books. She always loved when he read poems to her. Life was idyllic for the two of them.

Emerald possessed a photographic memory. She only had to be told or shown a thing once or twice at most and she could remember it or do it.

For Jimmy, having been so long on his own throughout his life and career, to have someone about the house who was so precious to him was indescribable. Before Emerald had arrived, if he took a long walk or a drive somewhere, when he'd come back everything would be in the same place in the house. Nothing would have been moved or disturbed. Everything would be exactly the same as he had left it. Now, even to know the kettle was on the boil as he returned home or to see that a book had been moved back to its shelf, were very special pleasures. Small things to other people perhaps, but important to someone who had never experienced them before – except when his nephew stayed over and then the place looked like a bomb hit it. Still, he loved Chris. His nephew was so sure of himself, not in an arrogant way but he had a confidence and an interest in everything.

One morning Jimmy sat at the breakfast table with a mug of tea in his hand, his mind wandering back to his childhood. He recalled the men from his village; tall, silent men. To get them to talk was like pulling teeth. He remembered when they came to visit his mother after his father was drowned in a storm along with four other fishermen. He remembered how they stood around the walls in the house like tall trees. Still, his mother got great comfort from their presence there. Maybe words were superfluous at those times.

'More tea?' asked Emerald.

'Well, if it's in the pot.'

She poured him a cup.

'Well, I hope you are pleased with yourself,' she said.

He looked at her blankly.

'That you can swim,' she added.

'Oh,' he laughed. 'It's a miracle that anyone could get an old dog like me to do something new, let alone swim.'

Emerald had insisted that they take to the water every day, whatever the weather. There was no doubt about it; he could swim a short distance and the childhood fear he'd had of the water was gone. Yes, he was very pleased with himself and grateful to her.

He pulled out a drawer of the cabinet and produced a parcel all wrapped up in fancy paper.

'That's for you!' He said, passing it across the table.

'For me?' Emerald loved to receive gifts. She carefully opened the wrapping without tearing the paper. Inside was a watercolour set, with paper and watercolour pencils. 'Oh, this is a wonderful gift.' She reached over and gave him a big hug.

'Careful,' he smiled. 'I don't want to spill this tea all over myself.'

She looked at all the different coloured pencils. 'Like the colours of the rainbow,' she said.

Jimmy had been giving her some lessons on how to paint and draw. It was second nature to her now. She explained that all mermaids and mermen are trained to be creative, to draw and paint as well as to sing and carve.

'Thank you again,' she said as she examined the fine-tipped brushes and the flat-shaped one. 'This can be my birthday present,' she smiled.

'Your birthday?'

'Yes, it's next Saturday, the 13th. I'll be seventeen.'

'Well, that calls for a bit of a celebration. I'm going to phone my nephew to see if he's back. He travels so much these days. He was trained in computers, but he gave it all up to pursue a career in music. He's twenty-eight or twenty-nine, I don't remember. I'm sure he'd love to meet you. He plays the flute and sings. Last time he was touring Europe with the band, what's it called now? Wait a minute, he gave me one of those CD things from their first recording. To tell you the truth I've never listened to it. Oh, but he's good, very talented. He's played for me on many occasions. Where is it? Oh yes.' He picked up the disc. 'How amazing,' he mused.

'What?' asked Emerald.

'The name of his band, it's called Emerald Road.'

Emerald smiled as they looked at the four faces staring from the photograph.

'They all look very serious,' said Emerald.

'Oh, that's just posing you know, the cool look. That's what's expected in the music world. He's not like that. In fact he has a wicked sense of humour. I hope he's there.'

He picked up the phone.

'He was due back last week. He'd usually get around to phoning me after a day or two.'

Emerald could see the old man's eyes light up as he spoke down the phone.

' . . . I have a friend visiting,' said Jimmy proudly. 'She's come to stay for a while . . . Yes, it's a she. What's so strange about that?' he retorted. 'Yes, I'm still a confirmed old bachelor and likely to remain so until the end of my days. Listen, cheeky, I would like you and your friends to come over on Saturday, as my friend Emerald,' He winked at Emerald, 'is celebrating her seventeenth birthday. Not seventy, seventeen. Come for tea, around six. And bring your musical instruments. We're going to have a bit of a celebration. Bye, see you Saturday.'

Jimmy put down the phone and rubbed his hands.

'We are going to have a birthday party for you, my young lady.' He laughed. 'It will be the first time there was ever a party in this place, but better late than never. I think I'll put the kettle on and we'll have some more tea.'

Emerald laughed.

'What's so funny about that?'

Chapter 15

Early on Saturday morning, before first light, Emerald took a walk along the quiet beach. This would be the first time she would celebrate her birthday without her family and friends of the watery kingdom.

The cliffs were silent. All the birds had fledged and had gone with the adult birds to live out at sea. The cliffs seemed so lonely without the constant raucous chatter of the birds. Emerald had never imagined she would ever get to know the land and love it so.

She watched the slow sombre flight of a grey heron flying low over the sea, before alighting near the estuary. There it began to stalk the shallow waters. Emerald remembered the evening she swam up the river with Dorad to get a glimpse of the nusham world, but she was so scared that night. Now it was as if she was a nusham and her life as a mermaid was a mere dream.

She climbed up to the top of the sand dunes and watched the first light of dawn break in the east. It was so beautiful to see the shafts of colour spread through the pearl grey sky. She had seen it hundreds of times before from the water and from small islands, yet she realised no two dawns were ever the same. Each new day brought new skies. Each day the sea was different. No bird flight was the same as yesterday. It might appear the same but it was new like the day.

Emerald lay in a sheltered spot in the dunes where she could hear the faint sound of the sea. She closed her eyes and in her mind she travelled back to her family and friends. She missed her life as a mermaid, and wondered if her sisters would remember that it was her birthday today. Were they forbidden to see her? Had the elders imposed a ban to prevent them visiting her, she wondered? Her mother could overthrow any ban if she wanted to. It was several months since Emerald had made the transition to nusham, but she would always be a mermaid in her heart.

She wondered was she fulfilling her mission? She didn't really know what her true mission was. To convince the nusham that what they were doing was wrong? In the village, the nusham seemed so kind to each other; they didn't seem to be destroying the sea or wild folk. Oh, she had encountered the occasional ignorant driver who had almost run her over crossing the road. But apart from that everyone she met was kind and considerate.

Yet the television programmes told a different story. Caved-in faces and skeletal bodies of famine victims or loud angry faces shouting at the screen. Fires. Wars. Murders. Pictures all showing a world in turmoil.

Emerald recalled one night having been captivated by the

television and seeing the colour pictures of wild folk flickering in front of her very eyes. Then later she remembered feeling so sick to her stomach as she watched some war raging somewhere, angry soldiers and blood-stained women and children strewn about the ground, that poor Jimmy had to help her to the bathroom. Since that time they watched very little television, the occasional wildlife documentary only or a movie. They preferred to read, listen to music, paint and carve.

Overhead, the honking sound of geese could be heard as they flew towards the estuary. Emerald decided to take a swim. She got to her feet, jumped from the sand dunes onto the soft sand and ran down to the sea. Wading in up to her waist she plunged into the water. It was so invigorating. She surfaced, turned on her back and floated, feeling the pull of the tide. Then she turned to look back at the shore where she had been sitting earlier. A kestrel hovered then flapped low over the line of the sand dunes.

The previous day Jimmy had shown her where part of the sand dunes was becoming eroded by the winds. He explained how he had collected discarded Christmas trees in the village and used them to help prevent damage to the dune system.

Suddenly Emerald felt something touch her feet lightly. She turned to see Dorad leap out of the water in front of her and perform several acrobatic feats, before coming to rest beside her.

'Dorad!' She threw her arms around him. 'Oh it's so good to see you. Let me give you a big hug. You remembered!'

The dolphin nodded then opened his beak. Emerald stroked his tongue and gums. He clicked.

'You have a surprise for me? Where is it?' she wondered.

He clicked again. She fingered below his tongue and found

a beautiful ring with a sapphire stone. Putting it on her finger she ran her hand over the water, then holding her hand to her face she exclaimed: 'It's beautiful.'

The dolphin told her to climb on his back. She gripped his dorsal fin and threw her leg over him. Then they were away over the waves just like it was before, Dorad increasing his speed and making it a challenge for Emerald to stay on.

Then he began to cruise with ease. She thought she heard her name being called. Turning, she could see her sisters, astride dolphins, heading over the waves towards her. Emerald shrieked with excitement. They leaped off their dolphins and swam to each other. They hugged and kissed and spoke loudly, unable to contain their excitement.

Jade and Azure explained that they were heading for the lighthouse and were going to leave birthday gifts for their sister on the rocks nearby. Emerald thanked them dearly as she opened the gifts hidden in scallop shells and seaweed bags. Azure's gift was a silver bracelet adorned with lovely designs of dolphins. Jade had given her shell-shaped earrings and her mother sent her a beautiful embroidered waistcoat.

'They're lovely presents,' said Emerald. She tried on the waistcoat, then put in the earrings and placed the bracelet on her wrist. 'Look at me!' she pulled a pose, Queen of the Sea, waving her arms. They laughed loudly.

They all swam to a quiet cove and sat on some seaweed-covered rocks. The dolphins circled about nearby. Jade and Azure began to feel her legs.

'What do you think?' Emerald asked.

'They don't look bad, for legs,' they sniggered.

They spent all the morning and most of the day catching up with all the news. Emerald enquired about her mother and father. She was told that they had gone to a summit that the old empress had called. She was picking up some terrible message from the seas, that something was going to put much of the sea world at risk.

'That's awful,' said Emerald. 'Does she know what it is?'

'No,' said Azure.

'Perhaps it's just fearful dreams of an old woman,' said Jade.

'What about the others who took the transformation rites?' wondered Emerald.

'We have no idea,' said Azure.

'It is rumoured some of them chose to become dolphins and orcas and communicate with the nusham that way, gaining their trust and confidence. We heard that from the white-sided dolphins, so it must be true,' added Jade.

'Anyway Mother and Father are gone along with the elders and delegates from the whales, dolphins, seals and other sea creatures who wish to attend. Mother and Father wished you a happy birthday and told us to be sure to bring you these gifts.'

'Ah, they're so sweet,' said Emerald.

'Mother has been so anxious for you. Everyday she says: "I wonder how my dear child Emerald is. I hope she is safe. I hope she's not too lonely. I hope the nusham are not being cruel to her." ' said Jade.

'Well, she does worry,' said Azure.

'When did they leave?' asked Emerald.

'Only a few days ago,' they replied.

'Everyone is so concerned about you,' said Jade. 'While you look like you are on vacation,' she teased.

'I'm having a birthday party tonight, I wish you could come,' said Emerald.

'We'd love to but we've no spare legs,' laughed Jade.

Emerald explained how kind the nusham was, and that she had met many more kind nusham who live nearby.

'Listen!' said Azure.

They could hear the sound of a fishing trawler. Hordes of scavenging gulls followed behind it in the hope of discarded offal or fish.

'We'd better go,' said Azure. They hugged each other and said they would meet again soon. Emerald climbed on to Dorad and they headed towards the land.

* * *

Jimmy was getting a bit anxious. Emerald had left before dawn without breakfast and it was now six o'clock in the evening. The guests would be arriving shortly. He scanned the beach with his telescope then looked out to sea. To his amazement he could see her on the back of a dolphin coming towards the shore.

At the same time he could hear a car pulling into the drive. It was Benny Browne and the other members of his group. Another minibus followed close behind. It was his nephew, Chris, with his band.

'Welcome back, young Christy,' said Benny, as he shook Chris's hand warmly.

Jimmy came out the side door of the house. He seemed in a bit of a flap. Emerald wasn't in the house and if any of them saw her out at sea what would he say? Then he thought about it for a moment and realised they couldn't see the beach from the road.

'Greetings uncle,' said Chris, pulling him close in a bear hug. 'This is my uncle, guys, Jimmy 'Sparrow' Talbot. He's called 'Sparrow' because he's so tiny,' said Chris.

'Listen to him!' laughed Jimmy. 'I'm taller than you, you little whippersnapper.' Jimmy tossed his nephew's curly hair. 'Have they no barbers in Europe?'

His friends laughed. Chris introduced them. 'This is Phil!'

'Howdy!' Phil replied.

'You can tell he's from the Lone Star state. You know Cormac.'

'Nice to see you again, Mr Talbot.'

'This is Jeff from London.'

'Good evening,' responded Jeff.

'And this is Osamu Yoshizawa. He's from Ireland.' They all laughed. 'No, he's from the land of the rising sun.'

Osamu nodded in a courteous fashion. After the introductions were over, Chris asked where was the birthday girl. Jimmy looked awkward. Then Emerald came out from the house.

'Right here!'

Emerald's and Chris's eyes locked on to each other. Chris was dazzled by her extraordinary beauty and her radiant complexion. He extended his hand and shook hers warmly. She thought he was the most handsome nusham she had seen, with his black curly hair and penetrating brown eyes.

'We decided to risk a barbecue. It's supposed to be a clear, dry evening, well, according to the weather people.' Jimmy said doubtfully, eyeing Benny.

'That sounds great,' said Chris.

Everyone helped organise tables and chairs and Chris took over the task of cooking the steaks and burgers.

'I like mine cremated,' said Benny. This brought loud laughter.

'He may be a star around the world, but here he's just one of the guys isn't that right, Jimmy?' said Paul the banjo player.

They all sat around and enjoyed the meal and the refreshments. Knowing Emerald did not eat meat, Jimmy had bought vegetarian burgers for her and she helped herself to the rice and salads. After a time a lovely cake was produced by Jimmy. It was circular with a lighthouse design decorated on it, and seventeen burning candles.

They started a chorus of *Happy Birthday*. Emerald smiled and Jeff took a photograph. Emerald continued to look at the colourful candles with their small flames dancing in the light breeze.

'You'd better blow those candles out soon,' said Jimmy. 'I'm dying for a slice of cake.' Emerald took the cue, inhaled a deep breath and blew them all out. Everyone applauded. Paper plates were produced with a Mickey Mouse design on them.

'Is this a kid's party?' asked Tim the bodhran player, teasing Jimmy.

'They're the only plates I could get, cheeky. Besides, it saves me having to do the washing up after you lot.' Jimmy handed Emerald the knife.

She hesitated. Chris took her hand and helped her cut into the cake and divide it up equally.

'I don't know about you lot, but I prefer cake with tea,' said Jimmy, holding the teapot in the air in his right hand.

'We'll all have tea,' Chris smiled.

Small presents were produced by the different people. Chris gave her a sweater with a humpbacked whale breaching on it. Jimmy gave her a watch. 'It's waterproof,' he added.

She thanked them all, saying she had received so many gifts today that she was spoiled. She then showed what her sisters and Dorad had given her. Luckily no one asked her who Dorad was. It was an anxious time for Jimmy. Then she showed them the waistcoat that was a present from her parents. They all looked in amazement at it.

'It's beautiful,' they remarked. Osamu examined it. 'If these gold threads and the pearls are real, then your family must be very wealthy, for this is worth a fortune.' He stared at the intricate work on the waistcoat.

'It's a theatrical waistcoat, like her comb. Her parents are in the music business,' blurted Jimmy. 'Ballet, I mean opera. More coffee or tea for anyone?' he continued, trying to change the subject.

'We've all had plenty,' said Benny. 'I'm stuffed to the gills.'

'You don't have gills, only fish have,' said Emerald.

'It's just an expression,' said Chris. 'Have you not heard it before?'

'How about some music?' said Jimmy to the others. 'That's the only reason I invited you lot here,' he teased.

Benny and his group took out their instruments, tuned them up and began to play. Then they coaxed Chris to sing an old Irish lament, which he did.

Emerald clapped enthusiastically. 'You are really good.'

'Well he should be,' retorted Tim. 'Isn't he making heaps of money selling all those CDs and tapes.'

'You put such feeling and conviction in the song,' continued Emerald.

'Time for a song, Jimmy,' called Benny.

Jimmy cleared his throat: 'Just because I've a famous nephew as a singer doesn't mean his poor uncle can sing. But I will have a go. This is called the *Connemara Lullaby.*'

He started to sing and everyone joined in the chorus. Emerald squeezed his hand warmly when he had finished. Chris watched in amazement.

'Now, we'll get Osamu to play us something.'

His Japanese friend smiled broadly and took out a wooden flute.

'This is a Shakuhachi. I have Chris playing it now and he's very good. Not as good as me,' he smiled, 'but good.'

'Get playing and stop blowing,' retorted Chris.

'Well, since we're on such a beautiful island by the sea I will play one of my own compositions. It's called *Nami* meaning wave. It's the story of a wave cut off from the ocean, left alone in a rock pool. It's a sad tune I wrote for my daughter Yoko who gave me the idea.'

Osamu started to play.

The sound was incredibly pure and moving. When he finished everyone applauded loudly. Emerald asked if he had written any words to accompany the piece.

'Well, it's funny you should ask. We were trying the lyrics out with several female singers. But they all got stuck on the phrasing, and singing the long passage without taking a breath. They say it's impossible to sing.'

'Could I try?' she asked.

Osamu looked at Chris who nodded a why not. He handed her the words. Jimmy began to get anxious.

Emerald scanned the paper, then put it down.

'Okay, I'm ready when you are.'

'You're ready?' said Osamu in disbelief. He began to play the first passage then gave her the nod to join in.

Emerald began to sing. She was word perfect and she took a breath at the right place and held the note. The sound seemed to rise and fall like the waves, touching all the right emotions with her amazing voice. There was such truth in her voice, such beauty.

Everyone was stunned into silence when she finished. Then Jimmy broke the mood: 'She always has that effect when she sings to people.'

Osamu grasped her hands. 'Thank you, that was truly incredible.' Jimmy smiled proudly and patted Emerald on the back.

Chris looked at her, then said quietly but forcefully: 'You are good.'

'Well, thank you,' said Emerald, in a coquettish fashion.

'No really, you've got it! You are the only one I've heard in a long time who can really use the voice. Were you trained?'

'Oh yes, we all practised singing from the time when we were small children.'

Jimmy stood up. 'Well, I hate to bring such a wonderful evening to a close. But these old bones of mine need to rest.'

Benny Browne looked at his watch. Nearly midnight. 'Time flies when you are having fun.'

Jimmy held Emerald by the arm and whispered: 'Be careful not to reveal too much. I know you are among friends but let's keep your true identity a secret. I say this not for me alone but for you.'

'I understand.' She kissed him goodnight on the cheek.

Chris and the Emerald Band were staying over; there was plenty of room in the old house. They said their goodbyes to the Village Fiddlers, who had really enjoyed the evening. They once again wished Emerald a happy birthday and said they hoped to see her in the Sailor's Wharf during the week.

Chris indicated to the others that he wanted to speak to the young girl alone. He invited her to stroll along the beach before going to bed. Emerald was delighted. She liked being in the company of so handsome a nusham. Jimmy watched from his bedroom window as Chris and Emerald made their way down towards the beach. They walked silently for a time with only the sound of the sea lapping to the shore.

Chris asked how she had come to know his uncle. She answered that she had met him by chance one night, but that she had often seen him foraging along the shoreline. He laughed.

'That's the word for it all right, foraging. He's the master beachcomber. He's been doing it all his life. His brother, my dad, says he's a collector of junk. Uncle Jimmy would always answer: "One man's junk is another man's treasure." '

'Where are your parents now?' asked Emerald.

'They moved to the south of France. My father took early retirement, sold up and moved. They're very happy there. I saw them last week. We've been on tour around Europe, I'm sure my uncle mentioned it.'

Emerald nodded.

'I used to walk along here as a child. I always imagined I was someone living between two worlds. I'd have one foot in the water and one on the land.'

Emerald wondered was there more to what he was saying.

'My uncle tells me you are a student of the marine,' he continued.

'You could say that,' Emerald responded, slightly on the defensive.

Chris stopped and looked at the moon hanging above the sea. 'It is a very beautiful night. The sea looks silver.'

'A silver tide,' said Emerald.

'It's a strange thing that our band is called Emerald Road and you should turn up.' Emerald stayed silent but looked warmly at him. 'Listen, I think you have the most wonderful God-given voice I've heard, I mean it.'

Emerald smiled: 'You haven't heard my sisters.'

'I have heard you . . . now I don't know what your plans are or whether you are in college or what, but I would love you to join our band. You would be a sensation.'

'Well, it's very kind of you to ask me,' said Emerald.

'It's not kindness; you would be doing us a favour. We're cutting an album in New York over the next few weeks. You could sing what you sang earlier, *Nami,* the wave. Then we can go on a world tour. I know you will be a smash . . . the audience will love you.'

'But I'm on a mission,' she said. 'I have to tell the nusham, I mean the people, to stop polluting and emptying the sea of its wild folk.'

Chris was taken somewhat aback by her words, then he retorted forcefully: 'Listen, if you believe you are on a mission, fine. You could end up on television and in live concerts. You could give out your message in between songs.'

'A millennium message to save the seas.'

'I love it; it would work.' Chris could not contain his excitement.

'They are not my words,' said Emerald in a serious tone. 'They are Grandmother Nature's words.'

'Well, whatever . . . Gaia call it what you will.' He placed his hands on her shoulders. 'Please consider it. It will benefit us all and give people the chance to hear your glorious voice.'

'Let me think about it,' said Emerald. It's all been too much recently. I feel like a player in some mysterious game that I don't have any control over.'

'I understand, truly. One minute I was a whizz-kid computer guy, next minute I go on holidays and meet up with guys at a gig. Somehow I get a chance to sing and play with them. A year later we are cutting our first album in London. Now, eight albums later we've done a worldwide tour and now I'm a very rich dude! When I think about it, it's a bit mind-blowing. So I understand how you might be feeling. You sleep on it,' he said warmly.

'Thank you for the lovely evening,' said Emerald. She hugged him and ran back towards the house.

There was something mysterious about her that Chris couldn't quite figure out. She was certainly different from any girl he'd met before. It was as if she was harbouring some secret. He didn't want to probe, but he would like to know more about her. Taking out his mobile phone he checked for a signal, then phoned his producer, Harry Taffin.

'Ah Chris, how are you.' Chris told him he was fine and was walking a beach. There was laughter from the other end. 'Well, it's better than what I'm doing, watching some dire made-for-TV movie.'

Chris was congratulated on the success of his tour and told that his last album was number nineteen and rising in the US charts. Chris was delighted; he couldn't wait to tell the guys.

'Well, I was going to keep it a secret until we met, but since you called I thought I might as well give you the good news.'

Chris thanked hime again, but now he was more keen to discuss his new discovery. His producer seemed interested and asked what kind of voice Emerald had. Chris answered: 'Think of Sinéad O'Connor, Enya, and Maria Callas and you're getting warm.'

'Sounds impressive. I hope she's got a lot of anger,' his producer added.

'Well no, she's not that kind of performer.'

'Listen, Chris, you may be besotted by this girl's voice, you must be phoning me after midnight, but pretty singers are two a penny. You know that,' Harry pleaded.

'You'll have to meet her, Harry and listen to her singing. You'll want to sign her up immediately,' urged Chris.

'Well Chris, you know I don't do the signing up. Listen, I have a meeting with Mr L Sherman tomorrow. Why don't I talk to him and we can hop over and meet your new discovery. That's the best I can promise.'

'That would be great, Harry. Goodnight, and buy yourself a video machine, so you can watch something decent,' he teased.

Chapter 16

'I'm so pleased you think it's a good idea meeting these people from the music industry,' said Emerald.

'Well, I'm quite sure my nephew will not let them exploit you or make you sign any sneaky contracts.'

'I'm nervous meeting these people,' said Emerald. 'I don't know why.'

'I'll come too,' said Jimmy. Emerald gave him a big hug. 'It's a free meal, isn't it?' he laughed loudly.

When Emerald and Jimmy arrived at the restaurant Chris and the band were deep in conversation with two men. One was the band's producer Harry Taffin, the other was the chairman of Track Records, who had produced all the Emerald Road albums. They had many famous names signed up. As Emerald walked in they stood up to greet her and Jimmy. Chris did the introductions. Mr L Sherman was a big, heavy-set man with a bald head and thick-rimmed classes. He smoked a cigar.

'Chris tells me you have a lovely voice,' said Mr L (as he was known to the people who worked for him).

'None better,' Jimmy piped up.

'Chris also tells me you are big into the environment, saving the seas and all that,' he continued. Emerald nodded. 'That's good, not very original but worthy nevertheless.'

'It was Chris's idea, you know, that we come to the Oyster Fish Restaurant,' Harry Taffin quipped.

Suddenly a beautiful girl walked in, kissed Chris and sat beside him.

'Sorry I'm late, I had to get the later flight. I was on the phone all morning. You have a gig in Madison Square Garden in November.' This news was greeted with loud approval and congratulations. 'You have second billing.' Again a cheer.

'Last time it was "and others",' Jeff retorted.

'Well, you guys are hot, and you better stay that way.'

Emerald was introduced to Debbie, Chris's girlfriend. Emerald got the feeling Debbie didn't like her, but she was courteous. When they were ordering Emerald was asked what she would like. She ordered a vegetarian curry and the five lobsters in the tank. This took the others by surprise.

'Do you think you can manage to eat five lobsters?' asked Harry Taffin.

'Oh, I don't want to eat them,' said Emerald. 'Could you please put them in a plastic bag with water?'

'Certainly, madam,' said the waiter, rather puzzled.

'Weird,' remarked Debbie.

Jimmy laughed.

After the meal they agreed to visit a studio in the city the following day and do a demo of Emerald singing *Nami*. Jimmy undertook to have Emerald at the Bluebird Studio by nine o'clock the next morning. They said their goodbyes. Chris said he looked forward to recording with her. Debbie sat with her arms around Chris and called after Emerald: 'Enjoy your supper of lobsters.' Then was heard saying: 'You wouldn't want to bring her to lunch every day. The profits would be gone.' This brought a big guffaw from Mr L and Harry Taffin.

*   *   *

'Somehow I don't think we are going to have lobster for supper,' said Jimmy on the way home.

'No,' said Emerald. 'The lobsters were communicating with me throughout the entire meal, asking me to save them. They wanted to go back to the sea.'

They stopped near the pier on the way home.

'This is where they're from,' said Emerald removing the twine from their pincers.

Then heading down the steps to the water's edge she gently dropped the crustaceans into the sea. Jimmy sighed at all those tasty lobsters vanishing in front of his eyes into the dark waters.

'Oh, I forgot to tell you, I collected a blenny for your fish tank from the rock pool, and some algae,' cheered Emerald.

'Thanks,' said Jimmy dryly.

When they returned home the old man made a pot of tea. Emerald asked what he thought of her going into the band.

'Well, it's a wonderful opportunity, no doubt about it. You would get a chance to see the world and get your message across about what's happening to the seas.'

'Chris said the exact same thing,' said Emerald.

'Well, he's probably right,' he remarked. 'Though I have to say I don't really like those flashy suit merchants we had lunch with. Still, I know Chris and the others would keep a good eye on you. They know the ropes, so to speak,' Jimmy assured her. They sat silently for a time drinking tea and eating biscuits.

'I know I'm being selfish but I'm going to miss you if you leave to tour the world. For as sure as eggs are eggs when they hear your voice they will want more and more and I wouldn't blame them one bit.'

'Grypus said something similar,' she smiled.

'See! We are all enchanted by you,' he said sadly.

Emerald stood up and wrapped her arms around his neck and leaned down on him.

'You are my only family on land. I will always return here if I do decide to go, but I'm still undecided. Will I be able to get my message across? I'm sure there have been others from the land people who tried and perhaps others from the sea.'

She seemed lost in thought as she recalled her grandmother's words: 'The folly of interfering with the sea, with their curtains of death drift nets, their chemical poisoning, their oil spills. The nusham are the major predator and destroyer of the sea, no doubt about it.'

'You have the words, young lady. If anyone can make a plea for the sea, you can.'

She hugged him more tightly. 'I'm only echoing the words of Grandmother Nature, the old empress and the other sea people.'

'We need to hear the words again and again until we learn to have respect for this God-given planet.'

She pulled out his handkerchief. 'Your nose is running,' she grinned. He blew his nose. 'I think I'll go for a swim. I can think much better in the water.'

'Go right ahead. I know you'll make the right decision.' He went to the door and watched her climb down the rocks, then he sat down and took out a book to read.

Later, checking his watch, he saw that it was nine minutes past nine. Since Emerald hadn't come back yet he decided to watch the news. He didn't like to watch it in front of her; it only upset her deeply.

'We bring you an extended news bulletin,' said a very grim newscaster. 'There has been public outcry throughout the world at the nuclear testing that took place in the early hours of the morning. Unconfirmed reports state that nine tests were repeated, one after the other, between Puerto Rico and the Azores in the Atlantic Ocean. No country has admitted to the testing, but there has been widespread criticism from world leaders. The president of the United States called it: "gross irresponsibility that could endanger millions of lives". Environmentalists called it a: "wipe out of the marine life" in the Atlantic Ocean. Remains of whales, seals, dolphins, fish and birds are scattered for miles. Millions of creatures have been literally burned alive. Several fishing fleets are reported missing. . . . It is feared a tidal wave of unimaginable proportions is building up in the boiling oceans and is heading straight for Ireland and Britain. It may even reach mainland Europe before its force is spent.'

Jimmy turned off the television and sat back in the chair in a state of total shock. There was nothing for it only to wait for the deluge. He began to think of all the people he knew, all the families, the children, heading for an untimely death. It wasn't fair. Suddenly he jumped up. 'I must warn Emerald!' He hurried out the door.

* * *

Emerald felt a terrible sense of foreboding, she couldn't understand why. Her body was rigid with fear. Floating on the water she turned around. In the distance she could see black clouds racing across the sky. The winds suddenly began to pick up. Her heart started palpitating. Birds flew overhead on panicked wings. Seals began to haul themselves onto the shore.

Shoals of fish flared past her. Creatures seemed to be fleeing in terror. Walls of water began to build up. But why she wondered?

Suddenly Emerald was grabbed by the arms. She screamed.

'It's only us, dear sister.' Her two sisters surfaced from below. 'A terrible thing has happened. We must get to the palace to safety, otherwise we'll be dashed onto the rocks.'

The winds were increasing all the time.

'Why is the sea so angry?' said Emerald.

They sobbed loudly.

'Because the nusham have captured the light and made the death bombs with it. Now, come on,' they demanded.

'I don't understand,' said Emerald.

The seaspray lashed their faces. 'We didn't want to tell you here, but Mother and Father are dead, as well as the old empress and all the delegates.'

'Dead?' said Emerald. 'All dead?'

'Yes, destroyed by the cursed nusham. Now, come on. There's no time to lose. The elders who stayed behind have held an emergency meeting and voted you Empress of the Sea.'

'Me?' said Emerald. 'But why me?'

'We don't know.' said Jade.

All we know is that if there is no empress there will be anarchy. The elements will be completely out of control.' Lightning illuminated the sky. 'We're nearing a total disaster. The tsunami is coming,' said Azure. 'The wave of death.'

'Now please come,' pleaded Jade.

'What about the nusham who live on the land?' asked Emerald.

'What about them? They caused this disaster,' snapped Azure. 'Let them perish like the evil things they are.'

'No,' said Emerald. 'It wasn't these people.'

Waves washed over them in great force. Her sisters bobbed back up.

'This is our last time to ask are you coming.'

'No!' said Emerald.

'Well, we cannot stay.'

They hugged each other and the two sisters headed off for the safety of the mermaid palace.

The winds howled and the sea raged.

Emerald thought she could hear her name being called. She turned and saw a dark figure trying to steady himself in the wind. It was the old man. She swam towards him and was scooped up by the waves and flung towards the shore. Jimmy was on the ground, soaking wet, being lashed by the driving rain and wind.

'Thank God you are all right. Come in for shelter,' he pleaded.

'No Jimmy, I cannot.' She helped him up to the lighthouse. 'Stay here tonight,' she begged him.

He fumbled in his pockets and found the keys to the small front door. She helped him in. The winds and waves were raging and lashing the lighthouse.

'They cannot blame this on El Nino. I saw it on the news,' he sobbed. 'They were doing some kind of nuclear tests.'

'Please stay here and keep warm,' she ordered him. 'I know what I have to do,' she cried.

'Don't go back out,' he pleaded. 'You'll only get yourself killed.'

She hurried outside and was nearly flung over the rail by the force of the storm.

The rain and wind hissed and roared. Emerald fought her way back to the water's edge. She forced her body past the buffeting waves. She was violently tossed about but she pushed on, groping her way in the thunderous dark deep waters. Columns of water built up beside her. The waves crashed down on her. Her body ached.

The waves continued to beat at her body. She began to feel faint. The water sizzled. The storm clouds swirled overhead.

'Dorad! Dorad!' she cried for help. Screams of frightened gulls among the black clouds drowned out her voice. 'Dorad,' she called feebly.

She ached all over but she forced herself onwards in the boiling waters. She knew her sisters would find safety in the caverns of the palace. But her land friends were living in the shadow of death and could do nothing about it. She believed only she could do anything. Then there he was alongside her.

'Dorad!' she cried, hugging him and climbing on him. 'No, Dorad. I don't want to go to the palace. Take me to where the wave is at its most vicious.'

Dorad moved at great speed over the waves. Emerald's body was bruised and battered by the driving wind and rain. The sky thundered and the wind screamed. It made her shudder but they pressed on. Her grandmother had once told her that wild folk could communicate with the sea. She knew her grandmother could, but could she?

Then she saw it, rising like a giant monster from the depths. Growing in stature every moment, a huge volume of water forming a gigantic wave, a spectre of death, fuelling itself with all the forces of nature before it would make its deadly attack on the land people. It was justified. Had they not created the monster? They who sow the wind, reap the whirlwind.

Emerald trembled in awe at this massive wave. She had never seen anything like it before. It rose, restless. It was ready to wage war and destroy all in its path. There was a terror and a grandeur about it. She stood in front of the jaws of death.

Emerald thought she could hear a voice sounding in her head. Saying how dare she try to impede the tsunami, the wave of destruction. She could see that the tsunami was ready to unleash its full energy. A deadly ominous silence descended, charging the atmosphere before the final deadly onslaught. It was now or never, she thought. She raised up her arms as if to make a plea to the great mystery that gave life a chance in the first place.

Becoming conscious of a small sudden movement behind her, Emerald looked over her shoulder. There was old Grypus, the orca and Lutra. They moved alongside her and Dorad.

'Why, dear friends? It isn't safe . . . none can withstand the tsunami.'

'Friends we are,' said Grypus. 'And we'll stick together through thick and thin.'

Emerald smiled sadly. 'My dear foolish friends, I thank you for your company on this night of nights.'

Forked lightning tore across the sky and thunder began again. The tsunami began to throb, moving up and down like a great monster rousing itself. The thunder was its yawns.

Emerald rubbed Dorad on the forehead, then with outstretched arms she began to sing to the giant wave. She sang with all her being. Of the loss of beauty in destruction, of the sacred mystery that was life. She sang of the primordial, of the elements, of the infinite varieties of life forms, of the celestial spheres. Her message was the message of love, of courage to forgive, of tides of renewal. Her voice radiated an energy that seemed to envelop the sky and the water. Its power was in its splendour. There was a vibration from it that her friends could feel in the core of their very beings.

She stood fearless against the giant wave and poured out her heart in words and sounds of love and compassion. Her voice seemed to mingle with the water.

Gaping holes began to appear in the wave, like a waterfall that met some obstruction. The level of the wave had seriously diminished. Emerald opened her eyes and could see the wave was contracting. She summoned up all her strength and sang more brilliantly than before. It was as if everything was touched with a fragrant breeze.

Suddenly the wave collapsed in on itself . . . and the sea became calm. Soon the storm was gone, completely blown away. A glorious afterglow of a sunset appeared over the horizon and an exquisite serenity could be felt. Manx shearwaters flew lightly over the wavelets.

'You did it,' said Grypus. 'You beat the tsunami.'

Emerald slowly lowered her arms and collapsed backwards. Her friends circled her and supported her in the water. There was no movement from her, except the sea gently brushing off her beaten and bruised body. It was as if she had put all her strength and being into the song. Her heart seemed broken. They stared in stunned silence. After a time, the orca offered to carry her back to the mermaid palace. Emerald was laid across the orca and in processional mood they slowly journeyed to the great cavern.

Chapter 17

Jimmy Talbot sat huddled in the basement of the lighthouse. He couldn't believe that he had actually fallen asleep during that terrifying storm. The bible lay open where he had been reading about Jesus calming the storm. It had been of great comfort to him during the night when the rain, waves and wind lashed and battered at the lighthouse. He thought it was the end. It should have been, that was what was predicted. Slowly he got to his feet. He was so stiff. His body ached. He stretched, then thought of poor Emerald.

He hurried up the stairs and scanned the waters with the telescope. There was no sign of any movement. It was a beautiful calm day and a lantern sun hung in the sky. The beach was covered with debris washed in by the storm; enough beachcombing for a month.

Jimmy couldn't believe his eyes. By some miracle his house and the lighthouse were still standing. As he made his way to the house he was delighted by the sight of a number of small songbirds flitting about in the bushes of his small garden. He grabbed his binoculars. There was a stray nightingale, a blackcap, a desert wheatear and a sleepy scops owl. He quickly wrote them down in his notebook. It cheered him up briefly but soon he began to think about Emerald again. Then the phone rang.

It was his nephew Chris. 'Thank God you're all right Uncle Jim,' he gave a sigh of relief down the phone.

They talked a lot about the nuclear testing and the threat of a tidal wave.

'Thank heavens it didn't happen. It shows how the experts

can often get it wrong,' said Chris. Then he asked to speak to Emerald.

Jimmy said sadly he didn't know where she was. That she had gone out for a swim the previous evening and had never returned. There was a long silence. Chris suggested calling the police. Jimmy could hear how upset his nephew was. He suggested they should meet and talk about her face to face and not over the phone.

'That would be lovely,' said Chris sadly. 'She was such a beautiful singer and a lovely person.'

Then he explained that the recording demo was cancelled and that the band members were now flying to New York with Mr L. who wanted them to do some TV work and promote the new album. Chris promised he would contact his uncle when he returned home from the Big Apple.

* * *

Several days later Jimmy faced the outdoors again. He had picked up a bad cold which had kept him indoors for nearly a week. He blamed the night of the bad storm and grumbled to himself. He never got a cold, except this one, and it knocked him for six and made him feel weak and tired.

But he felt a lot better on this day. He was well wrapped for the elements. A fresh breeze was blowing in off the sea. He walked along the beach and to his amazement saw what looked like a carved piece of driftwood. He picked it up. No seaweed or barnacles on it. He held it to his face. It felt cold to the touch. It was a carved ivory figurine that looked old, probably Victorian, he decided. What a find! It must be quite valuable.

He was engrossed in examining his find when he heard a voice from the sea. 'Beachcombing, are we?' He quickly turned to see Emerald half submerged in the water.

'Emerald! Emerald! Is it really you or are my eyes playing tricks?'

'It's really me,' she smiled. 'Do you like your present?'

'This is from you?' he asked. She nodded. 'I love it.' He kissed it, tears escaping from his eyes. 'I thought . . . well you know what I thought.'

'I nearly was, but thanks to my sisters who nursed me back to health and to my friends . . .' she gestured. Grypus bobbed up from under the water and snorted. 'This is Grypus.' The seal snorted again. 'And this is Lutra.'

The old man was amazed to see the leathery turtle circle her. 'Dorad you've seen before.' The dolphin clicked several times. 'And out there with the big black fin is an orca, a new friend.'

'Come and give me a hug,' Jimmy pleaded. 'I missed you sorely.'

'I'm afraid if you want a hug you'll have to come closer.' He looked puzzled. Emerald pulled herself to the shoreline. His eyes widened. He could clearly see her mermaid's tail.

She had become a mermaid again! He could hardly believe his eyes. A real mermaid lying on the beach. She still looked as beautiful as ever. He bent down and kissed her on the forehead.

'You should really be bowing down to me,' she smiled. 'I've been crowned Empress of the Sea.'

'Well you deserve it,' he said wiping his eyes. 'I'm so pleased you're alive. And all right. What happened with the deadly tidal wave?' he asked.

'Oh, I had words with it,' she said flippantly.

'What about the mission?' he enquired.

'I think the nusham are going to have to learn by themselves. They have the choice. To love the world or to violate it. If they learn to understand, then love will follow. The other is the road to destruction.'

'There is an old Irish saying,' said Jimmy. '*Dóchas, liaigh gach anró*. Hope, the physician of all misery.'

'I'd better go now,' said Emerald as she eased herself into the water.

'Will I ever see you again?' he asked sadly.

'I'm an empress, so on certain occasions, I may decide to make the transformation. I have the secret words.' Then she added lightly: 'But when I do call I'll expect the kettle on and it won't be tea I'll be after but hot chocolate like on the first night.'

'You can count on it, I will always be ready for you.'

Emerald climbed onto the dolphin, blew the old man a kiss and they were away over the waves.

Jimmy Talbot watched them disappear among the distant waves back to their watery kingdom.

* * *

THE SEA TRILOGY

Look out for other books in THE SEA TRILOGY

- *Saoirse, the Grey Seal*   - *When the Sea Calls*

The Sea Trilogy

DON CONROY

Saoirse
the Grey Seal

MENTOR

DON CONROY

**The
Mermaid's Song**

MENTOR

DON CONROY

WHEN THE SEA CALLS

MENTOR